The Song in the Night

Qazi Fasih was born in 1952 in the small town of Kohat in the Khyber Pakhtunkhwa province of Pakistan. He studied medicine at Khyber Medical College and was elected Literary Secretary of the College Students' Union. He went on to specialize in surgery and is a practising Urologist. He has written over twenty stories for Pakistani national television that focus on the country's social issues.

The Song in the Night

QAZI FASIH

Published by
Rupa Publications India Pvt. Ltd 2018
7/16, Ansari Road, Daryaganj
New Delhi 110002

Sales centres:
Allahabad Bengaluru Chennai
Hyderabad Jaipur Kathmandu
Kolkata Mumbai

Copyright © Qazi Fasihuddin 2018

This is a work of fiction. Names, characters,
places and incidents are either the product of the author's
imagination or are used fictitiously and any resemblance to any actual person,
living or dead, events or locales is entirely coincidental

All rights reserved.
No part of this publication may be reproduced, transmitted, or stored in a retrieval
system, in any form or by any means, electronic, mechanical, photocopying, recording
or otherwise, without the prior permission of the publisher.

ISBN: 978-93-5304-114-4

First impression 2018

10 9 8 7 6 5 4 3 2 1

The moral right of the author has been asserted.

Printed and bound in India by Gopsons Papers Ltd.

This book is sold subject to the condition that it shall not,
by way of trade or otherwise, be lent, resold, hired out, or otherwise circulated,
without the publisher's prior consent, in any form of binding or cover
other than that in which it is published.

To my Mamaji, Qazi Hameeduddin,
who introduced me to literature

One

They came from near and afar. Leaving their humble abodes at the break of dawn, the villagers walked long distances and hopped onto vehicles travelling in the direction of the town where the moot was to take place. They had adorned themselves with colourful caps and shawls, but their sunburned faces and gnarled fingers spoke of the gruelling lives they lived. Amongst them were farmers, fishermen, artisans and shopkeepers; simple folks from the nameless villages and hamlets that dotted the sprawling Indus Delta. Many amongst them had borrowed from friends and families to bear the cost of the journey. Their women had prayed for them when they departed, handing them red rice, flatbread and murky water in plastic bottles as sustenance for the journey. Some had pooled money and hired pickups and trucks. Others simply walked the distance.

During their journey, they engaged in heated discussions about their languishing lands and the stand their leaders should take. They were wary of their antagonists, who were educated people, but confident in themselves because they were the true sons of the delta and knew it well. Their forefathers had lived there for centuries and reckoned with the fury of the river and the wrath of the sea. Generations of ancestors had survived the to-and-fro struggle between these two rivals and borne the harshness of nature. Their descendants had managed to eke out a living with the anachronistic equipment and methods passed down to them. Now there was a clear danger to the few resources they had. They had risen to thwart that danger.

The river Indus, born on a Tibetan plateau, meandered through many a mountain and plain during its descent. It braided into numerous creeks and rivulets before its rendezvous with the ocean, giving rise to mudflats and swamps. It brought fertile alluvial soil when it flooded and pushed the sea back, regaining land for cultivation. The delta had seen glorious days in the past but was languishing now. Jannu, now leading a contingent of fishermen of the lake and shouting slogans with great zeal, had seen the degradation in his lifetime.

'When I was a child, my grandfather told me wonderful stories about our land,' an old man travelling with Jannu reminisced aloud as the pickup they were travelling in stopped to allow the engine to cool, and the discordant voices ceased.

'There were thick tamarisk forests for miles and miles along the banks of our river,' the old man went on. 'The plains had luxurious growth of grass and shrubs. Further down there were the evergreen mangrove forests in the swamps,' the old man paused while the others waited. They wanted him to continue. 'These swamps were good breeding places for shrimp and fish, of which there was no dearth. The boats never came back empty as they do now. There used to be abundant fodder for animals and the herdsmen didn't have to travel far. Milk and butter were cheap.'

Jannu interrupted the old man to talk to the driver. 'Why don't you get this thing moving?'

'I am waiting for the engine to cool down a bit more. You had asked me to take ten people for you and then you brought twenty,' the driver replied, pouring water into the radiator. 'Be patient. You can get busy with the fairy tale the old man is telling,' he smirked.

Jannu returned his impatient gaze towards the old man.

'My grandfather used to tell me that there was even a rice husking mill to which the farmers sold their crops. Arabs used to come in their dhows to buy camels and coal and take them across the sea,' the old man said.

'Now you are exaggerating,' a young man laughingly objected.

'No, I am not. It was exactly so a century ago,' the old man insisted.

'Then what happened? Why have all the trees and the grass vanished?' an angry companion of Jannu asked in exasperation.

'They made canals and bridges upcountry and took away the water of the Indus. Now our river is meek and rarely flows in fury. It is not the same Indus that used to be,' the old man mourned and fell into a melancholic silence.

'And now they want to dig a canal and bring us poisonous water,' Shani, another of the men, said angrily, grinding his teeth. 'We will see how they do it.'

They travelled the rest of the distance in silence. Soon the big tents and canopies and the crowds of people who had come to protest the canal became visible. Jannu grabbed Shani's arm and shook him in excitement.

'We made it, Shani. Look at the crowd!'

It had been an arduous journey. Jannu and his companions had worked tirelessly for this day.

Two

Jannu was a scrawny, middle-aged fellow with grizzled hair who lived in a bush house by the edge of the vast sweet-water lake. His home was some distance away from the village where the rest of his folk lived. He was a fisherman by trade and was known for his sagacity. He worked at the lake from dawn to dusk in his sailboat to catch as many fish as he could. His boat and his fishing net were old and needed repair on a daily basis but he treasured them. Jannu lived with his wife, Nooran, a carping, old woman ever complaining about his incompetence. They had two children, a seventeen-year-old boy and a very pretty fifteen-year-old daughter called Marvi. The boy, named Wali, had refused to pursue Jannu's profession and would rarely help his father in the daily travails of earning a living. Near the house, there was a patulous neem tree near, where the children spent their days. Its trunk had bifurcated and branched in a way that provided a couple of comfortable places to sit. In addition, they had secured a hammock between the branches and often spent hot afternoons lying in the hammock. The family had managed to live off Jannu's meagre earnings and had become used to a life of deprivation.

Jannu still remembered the day when he was wading in the mangrove swamps for shrimp and caught sight of a few people from the city. They called him and offered to pay, if he agreed to help them with planting mangrove saplings. Jannu happily agreed to a wage of ten rupees per sapling and worked diligently that day. Later, when they sat sipping tea, Jannu could not resist asking them.

'Why are you doing this?' he said.

'Have you not noticed that these forests are shrinking with every passing day?' a man named Arif replied.

'Of course, we have observed it and mourned it,' Jannu replied.

'Well, we don't want this to happen,' Arif told him, and explained that they were a volunteer group working to save the coastline from degenerating further. 'Now they are going to dig a canal that will drain water from the waterlogged lands upcountry and bring it to the sea,' Arif informed him.

'So?' Jannu did not see the harm in it.

'There are many sugar mills back there and their effluents will drain into the canal. Moreover, all the pesticides and chemicals they spray over the crops will be washed into the canal and by the time the water reaches here, it will be like poison for all the plants and the grass. The canal will poison your lands and your life.'

The men had talked to him in detail and Jannu had listened intently.

'You, the folks of this area, should raise your voice against this canal and pressurize the government to give up the project,' Asif had concluded in an ominous manner.

His words continued to bother Jannu, who had a sleepless night. The following day, Jannu talked to his fellow fishermen. Some did not pay heed, but a few understood what Jannu was telling them. The effects of the poisonous water on their livelihood could be devastating. They joined him in his effort to educate others and together they visited all the villages around the lake to talk to people. In a couple of weeks, Jannu had gathered significant support. He became a well-known man, and started enjoying the transition from anonymity to comparative fame. But Nooran's bickering intensified at this waste of time. She was concerned about losing the daily pittance her husband earned as he donned the cloak of a leader. Jannu had hoped that his son Wali would take his place, but Wali had flatly refused. He threatened to leave if his parents remained adamant about the issue. They had a bitter discussion and Jannu ended up blaming Marvi for spoiling her brother. She used to wash his clothes, massage oil into his scalp while he dozed and perform all his chores with alacrity. She refused to eat if Wali had not eaten, and didn't sleep until he had returned home. Ironically, Marvi's fawning attitude did little to endear her to her brother, but earned her the ire of her parents for the insolence of their son. Unable to scold his impertinent son, Jannu vented his anger on Marvi, who stood silently with tears in her eyes.

Jannu was not a man to give in. He started planting mangrove saplings early in the day and continuing his awareness campaign in the latter part of the day. Fortunately, Arif would now take him in his jeep and so he didn't have to walk long distances. They went from village to village, where they sat with villagers in circles on the ground and scratched maps in the mud with sticks, explaining the course of the canal and the damage it would do. They gained increasing support as the days passed. The disquiet began spreading among the people like a contagion. The issue became a subject of conversation while men were at work and around hearths in homes. The reactions of the people varied in intensity. The old did not have enough verve for practical protest, but the young arranged themselves in groups and began attacking government property in regular inland forays. Instances of arson and looting started finding space in newspapers and even in electronic media. As the unrest intensified, it raised hackles in the relevant circles. Apart from the banks financing the proposed project and a few government officers, two individuals were following the developments with keen interest.

One was Kamal Rizvi, a civil engineer by profession and a man of pragmatic disposition. He had rapidly risen in his profession, founded an engineering company and made himself its CEO. It was his company that had won the contract to dig the canal after the adroit wheeling and dealing of its chairman. Having won the lucrative contract, Rizvi returned to his office and sat smugly as his engineers and heavy machinery rolled into the region. He had hoped for a quick completion of the project, so he could pack up and return to collect his wages. Now there was news of unrest amongst the people of the region and they were making a nuisance of themselves. Although Rizvi was confident that the movement had no chance of success because of lack of effective leadership, he remained anxious. The messy grassroots movement was turning out to be more tenacious than it first appeared. He discussed the matter with his aides and was advised to wait and watch. That was what he decided to do.

Three

The other person keenly following the developments was already on the prowl. His old but well-maintained Land Cruiser slowed down to turn onto a dirt road. The man behind the steering wheel impatiently looked at the vast swathes of land in front of him and desperately wished he had not given up smoking. It had been a long drive from the port city to this desolate hinterland. He had passed many hamlets and honked at throngs of nude children bent on blocking his way. Throughout his journey, he had not come across a single school or a hospital. He had seen small-time farmers working in their fields and been inundated by beggars whenever he stopped to ask his way. The unending manifestations of poverty gave him a sadistic pleasure. This was the type of populace that could be readily inflamed and roused to violence. Comrade Haider was adept at working with such people.

He was an erstwhile politician who had become redundant when the epicentre of the ideology he propounded collapsed. He had been an ardent champion of the proletariat as a student leader. He had shot to prominence due to his incendiary speeches against imperialism and become popular as an intrepid champion of the cause of the poor. This had endeared him to puppetmasters inside and outside the country who put him on a regular payroll. He grew a beard that covered only his chin, twisted his moustache into handlebars and tied his hair in a ponytail. He also took to chain-smoking. His style in those days became a dernier cri for aspiring Reds as he took on the status of a celebrity. This was many years ago. When the ideology he preached collapsed, he was left jobless. Over the years, his hairline receded and his ponytail thinned. He had to give up smoking on the advice of his doctor as he had developed chronic bronchitis. The flow of stipends he had been receiving from across the border dried out and he had to dip into his savings. He took to small-time contracting to earn a living. His brand of activism was overtaken by a different political credo, one marked by deception and new players from feudal classes and industrial elites. Nevertheless, nostalgia continued to haunt him. The news of the unrest in the delta region presented him with one last opportunity, and he jumped into activity.

The dirt road finally came to a boscage of stunted trees and thorny bushes. He consulted his hand-drawn map and stopped his vehicle when he saw the bush house near a neem tree. A girl emerged from the thicket, chasing her two goats. Comrade Haider called out to her. The girl hesitated for a while but then turned to walk towards him with a grace uncommon at her age. As she came close, he was taken aback by her charming face. An affectionate smile came to his lips.

'Do you know a man called Jannu?' he asked.

'I do. He is my father,' the girl replied in a sonorous voice.

The man heaved a sigh of relief. 'Run and tell him someone has come to see him,' he said to her.

The girl nodded her head and hurried toward the house, the

goats trotting along in front of her. After a few moments, Jannu emerged from the house, his curious stare fixed on the stranger. The man turned off his vehicle and stepped down, extending his hand.

'My name is Comrade Haider. That is a lovely child you have,' he said, warmly shaking Jannu's hand.

Jannu brought him to the cot under the tree and asked Marvi to bring a hot cup of tea for their guest. He then asked Comrade Haider about the purpose of his visit. Haider began with a detailed account of his political career and his achievements for the cause of the poor. Jannu listened intently, occasionally nodding his head in appreciation. To Haider's pleasure, Jannu recollected his role in the farmer's movement against a dam that was planned upriver. Then Haider came to the issue of the canal and the reservations of the people of the delta. But when Jannu began to tell him about their movement, Haider interrupted him.

'The damage to government property that your boys are doing cannot go on for long. Soon, the culprits will be identified and taken to task. We have to demonstrate our potential in a more convincing manner. That is where you need me,' he said.

Jannu was soon convinced that he needed Haider's participation. He excused himself and loudly called for his son. A few moments later, a frowning Wali emerged from the house. Haider noticed the swagger in his gait and his angry mien and smiled. Boys like him were the fodder of choice for the kind of movement he had in mind. Jannu asked Wali to run and call Moti, the compatriot who was Jannu's closest neighbour. Wali grudgingly turned to obey.

Four

It was dark and Bachal was sitting on his favourite perch, a swing chair in the veranda of his garish mansion. He had downed the fourth glass of his beloved amber-coloured liquid and was beginning to feel the effect. His chosen vassal, Mithal, sat nearby on the floor, holding his own glass of the amber-coloured drink, courtesy of his master. Bachal always loved to talk his heart out to Mithal during these carousing sessions and did so in pleonastic language. Mithal, though a good listener, understood only part of his master's discourse, but never failed to grasp the message he wanted to convey.

Mithal was no ordinary servant. He belonged to a pedigree of loyal servants who had served Bachal's forefathers generation after generation. Mithal had been allocated to Bachal since childhood and had been pandering to his wishes for as long as he could remember. His servitude had reached the point where he could hear before his master spoke and comply before he was commanded. He was sharp-witted and had a good sense of humour. Over the years, he had become the de facto ruler of Bachal's suzerainty, and had proved his worth by remaining unconditionally loyal to his master.

He protected Bachal's wealth with impeccable honesty and was unforgivingly harsh towards the people who tried to nibble at his possessions or reputation. He was amply rewarded for his services, and Bachal was never frugal in taking care of him and his family.

Bachal was a seventy-eight-year-old landlord whose forefathers were awarded vast swathes of land in return for their services to the British crown. Despite his age, he was in good health and still not affected by diabetes or hypertension. He had four sons who looked after their share of his lands and lived in separate mansions of their own. A few years back, Bachal's fourth wife died and he was left alone in the big house. He took to politics for entertainment and was soon admitted into the highest echelons of political players. Still, his loneliness did not go away, and of late, he was beginning to repine for the scent of a woman, that too of a young woman. Satisfying this desire proved to be a more formidable task than he had expected. Twenty or so years ago, many families would have been happy to include him amongst them as their son-in-law, but the spread of education and visual media in society had rapidly changed the thinking of people. The stacks of printed papers in his vault were beginning to lose the battle against printed papers in books.

'Old age is a bad stage of life,' he said.

'Why do you say that, master?' Mithal responded immediately.

'By now, I have explored all that has intrigued me. I have achieved whatever I could and abandoned the quest for what was beyond me. The euphoria of success and the frustration of defeat, both proved to be temporary,' he continued as Mithal listened. 'In this river we call life, the result of a valiant struggle against, and the less glorious attitude of submission to, the force of the waves has proven to be no different. The river takes you where it is supposed to take you. The final result is the same, whether you fight or give in,' he paused.

'Yes, master,' Mithal urged him to continue talking.

'I have wrapped up most of the concerns of my life and only have to wait,' he smiled bitterly.

'Wait? Master?' Mithal asked. 'Wait for what?'

'Death, Mithal. What else?'

'Don't say such things, master,' said Mithal as his eyes welled up.

'I have to wait. Wait like a lonely traveller for the bus to arrive and take me to the faraway place veiled in darkness. This is the only road I will take, like everyone before me, because my choices are limited by time.' He looked at Mithal whose cheeks were wet now. Abruptly, Bachal changed his tone to a cheerful one. 'I may as well get busy while I wait. I want you to find me a woman, a young woman who can take me back to the crossroads from whence I came and show me other possibilities.'

'I will, master, I will,' Mithal said, heaving a sigh of relief. 'I have done my homework, master, and selected someone who can make you forget the analogy of the road and the bus,' he added, pleased with himself for his forethought.

'Oh really? Describe her to me,' Bachal sprang to life.

Mithal paused to find the right words and then spoke in a dreamy voice. 'She is still a child, but she has grown tall and graceful for her age. She has black hair tied in a long plait that lolls down to the small of her back, but two locks play around her face, which she shakes away every once in a while. Her face is round and her skin reminds one of a field of ripe wheat in moonlight, a conflation of light brown and milky white. Her wide black eyes are guarded by thick long lashes and arching eyebrows on an intelligent forehead. Her lips are pink and full, and her teeth white like pearls.'

Mithal was so pleased with his eloquence that he helped himself to another glass of the amber-coloured liquid from the bottle on the table. The description so ensorcelled Bachal that he was at a loss for words for many seconds.

Finally, he asked, 'And where is this jewel?'

'She lives by the lake near Dhoro Puran in the wetlands. But you will have to wait for a couple of years if you want to marry her,' Mithal said.

'I will, Mithal. I will. But how can we see her?' Bachal asked.

'We will go on a goose hunt to the lake and we will be her father's guests. He is a fisherman and he would be honoured to have you,' he told Bachal.

'Make arrangements, Mithal. I would love to go on this goose hunt,' he finally said and staggered back towards his bedroom.

Five

Jannu had a long meeting with Comrade Haider. Moti joined them after a while and they discussed the issue of the canal in detail. Comrade Haider was served red rice and gravy of dried fish for dinner. They continued their discussion until late in the night. The voluble Comrade Haider edified them about the difficulties of a community uprising, stressing that complacency had to be resisted until their goals were achieved. They finally decided to visit as many villages as possible the next day and introduce Haider to all the stalwarts of the movement. As Marvi prepared a bed for Haider, he kept throwing furtive glances towards her. He had rarely seen a more attractive young girl.

Comrade Haider endured a sweaty sleepless night, inundated by a cloud of mosquitoes and bothered by regurgitation of the fish curry. It became cooler in the later part of the night when a steady breeze began to blow. He dozed off for a while only to be woken up by the persistent crowing of Jannu's rooster. He left the bed and decided to go to the lake to wash. On his way to the lake, he saw thick verdant growth of wild bush around the water and paddy fields beyond. Traipsing over dew-covered grass, he reached the lake, serene and still in the dim light of dawn. He saw flamingos hunting for a morning meal, standing in shallow water on one leg. The fishermen were unfurling their sails to leave for work and seagulls were hovering about the boats in anticipation. Far away in the sky, he saw a flock of geese approaching the lake in 'V' formation. The ethereal atmosphere held him in thrall for a long time.

He returned revitalized and ready for the day. Marvi brought breakfast and gave him a lovely smile which cheered him further. He smiled back affectionately and could not resist telling Jannu that he wished she were his daughter. Some time later, Moti also arrived and they embarked on their journey. Driving through the roadless bush, they visited one village after another. Some of the people they met warmly welcomed Haider into their fold while others were leery of him. Haider's power of persuasion brought the sceptics into line and a general consensus grew about his leadership. His experiences were too valuable to be ignored. In the final meeting, where all the leaders from the villages were present, the canal was discussed in technical detail. Haider was surprised to know that the illiterate villagers knew the precise details of the canal's design. They had the strongest objection against the final course of the canal, where the water was to flow through a tidal link and then fall into the sea. This segment of the canal went against the natural gradient of the flow and it was bound to flood the lands in high-tide season.

Together they chalked out a list of demands and agreed upon the dynamics of their movement. The first step was to hold a press conference at the press club in the port city. Different persons were allocated different tasks. Haider volunteered to arrange for the transport and preparation of banners. It proved to be an organized and well-conducted meeting resulting in concrete steps forward for the languishing delta. Haider, in his concluding remarks, congratulated them for their discipline and resolve to rise for the sake of their posterity. In return, he was thanked for his selfless devotion to their cause and full trust was placed in his leadership. An upbeat Haider, optimistic about the rebirth of his political career, embarked on a return journey to the port city. They had agreed upon a date for the press conference, a little late for Haider's liking but the villagers wished to delay it because they were preoccupied with preparation for the investiture ceremony of their spiritual leader, Pir Muazzam Shah. For them, nothing was more important than the holy event.

Six

Pir Muazzam Shah was a remarkable man from a long lineage of remarkable men. He was the scion of a family whose forefathers had migrated to this area to preach religion. He was an austere man of god, greatly revered by the people who came to find god but found him instead. When he died, he was buried in the village he had lived in all his life. His grave became a shrine and a destination for devotees to pay homage. The pilgrims paid respect in the form of cash too. When they came, they threw paper notes on his grave like confetti at a carnival. Every night the family member in attendance swept the floor with a broom, gathering the money in a heap and taking it home. The corpse of the holy man, after all, did not have much use for currency. Part of the money was used to build a mausoleum and the rest was used to buy land. Over the years, the family of the holy man had become a family of landlords, but they had been wise enough to maintain their spiritual facade. When they stepped into the realm of politics, the people voted for them happily and maintained their allegiance by voting for them ever after. Pir Muazzam Shah's ancestor's corpse would continue earning more money than did his living progeny. When one patriarch died, the honour was bestowed upon the eldest son. Pir Muazzam Shah's father had died only recently, and it was his turn to climb the throne.

He had planned his investiture on a grand scale. The ceremony was to be held on the large grounds in front of the mausoleum. In addition to a constellation of politicians in power, eminent people from all walks of life were invited. These included folk musicians, wrestling champions, poets, scribes and media tycoons. Then, there was an open invitation to all devotees and their families, including the fishermen who lived in villages around the lake.

People made special preparations for the day. As it drew closer, the cheerful atmosphere intensified. The villagers bickered with tailors for early hemming of their clothes and bought open silk flags with iconic white doves stitched upon them–symbols of the shrine and its message to the world. They had saved all year for this day; part of the money was for donations to the grave and part for their preparations. The children frolicked in jubilation and the grown-ups praised Pir Muazzam Shah in songs. Jannu had new dresses tailored for himself, Wali, Nooran and Marvi. In a rare show of affection, Marvi's mother gave her a yellow silk handkerchief too. Jannu had also gifted his wife and daughter two sachets of shampoo to wash their hair that day. For Wali and himself, he had bought a bar of soap and some perfume. The fishermen sailed daily into the lake with their families, singing praises of Pir Muazzam Shah in unison with the beat of drums every evening and competed in regattas. Emissaries of the Pir attended these ceremonies and bestowed their blessings on the people as a reward for their loyalties. Similar festivities were taking place in other villages too until the day of investiture arrived. Everyone went to bed early but few slept because of the excitement.

They woke up at dawn, wore their gaudy new dresses, and waving their green flags, they emerged from their homes. They joined together to make caravans travelling by camel and donkey carts. Apart from the villagers, a plethora of entertainers came to the carnival. Amongst them were folk musicians, dancers, fortune tellers, men with trained monkeys and parrots. Drug peddlers, con artists, pimps and prostitutes also came to do business. There were male dancers with long hair swirling interminably with beating drums hanging around their necks and eunuchs dressed as women. It was a protean gathering; everyone wanted a share of the Pir's blessings. The festivities took an early start. The devotees first visited the shrine and gave their donations, dropping them into locked boxes with narrow slits in the lid. Then they settled in groups in the vast arena, facing a garishly decorated stage with a throne flanked by less ornate chairs. A series of tents had been erected to provide shade and the ground was covered with cheap rugs. People from different villages chose places to settle down, Jannu's community also finding a corner of their choice. There was fun and frolic as contingent after contingent arrived.

Marvi and her friends decided to walk around and see the festivities. Coy and graceful, she walked hand in hand with her friends. They stopped by the fortune teller whose parrot traipsed over a row of cards and then picked one with its beak. Every time the parrot did this, the girls giggled and nudged each other. They stopped by the monkey man whose monkey fired his toy gun like a soldier. They stopped to watch the man unendingly whirling with a drum hung around his neck. One of the girls tried to copy him but became giddy and fell to the ground. They all laughed heartily. They took turns on the rotating wheel and were thrilled. They stopped to watch a magician who swallowed a rolled-up piece of paper and then produced it out of his nose and brought a pigeon out of his sleeve. All this time, Marvi had her yellow silk scarf around her neck. When they saw men serving rice, they decided to return, their hunger sharpened by the aroma rising from the large dishes. Halfway back, Marvi suddenly stopped.

'My scarf! I have dropped it somewhere,' she exclaimed and then without waiting, darted back in search of it. She disappeared into the crowd so quickly that none of her friends could catch up. She tried to retrace her footsteps, frantically looking around. She went to the swings and to the wheel. She asked the fortune teller and looked around the place where the man was still whirling with his drum around his neck. She was on the verge of losing hope when she saw a boy holding her scarf and smiling at her predicament.

'Are you looking for this?' he asked.

Her face lit up. She shook her head in the affirmative. He was a handsome boy with a sweet smile.

'You dropped it when you were at the swing,' he said nervously, his voice choking with emotion.

With her gaze fixed on the boy's face, she took a step forward and extended her hand to take it.

'Can I keep it?' the boy asked.

She looked at him a moment and then slowly withdrew her hand. For some reason she could not refuse.

'I will always remember your generosity,' he said.

Marvi had never before known the emotions that had overcome her. She wished for time to stop and the moment to become an eternity. But the voices of people and their physical presence nudged her to reality. She turned and, walking briskly, disappeared into the crowd. The boy tied the scarf to his left wrist.

The people were sitting in groups, bent over rice dishes

and eating the delicious meal. Marvi walked towards where her folks were sitting. When she arrived, she saw her anxious mother standing and scanning the throngs for her. She was visibly relieved when she saw Marvi.

'Sit and have some food and don't you disappear like that again,' she scolded her.

After the food was consumed and empty dishes heaped for flies to buzz over, the people turned their attention towards the stage. The investiture ceremony was soon to begin and the crowd was being asked to settle down over the public address system. They moved closer to the stage to get a better view; the hum of their voices refusing to die down. Marvi and her friends had managed to find a place in the front row; Marvi's heart still throbbing.

Soon, five bearded men marched onto the stage and sat on the row of chairs. Each one was garlanded and shown his chair as their names were announced. The drone emanating from the crowd briskly faded away in a show of reverence, as these were significant names in the spiritual world. Finally, the name of Pir Muazzam Shah was announced and the frantic devotees roared in a spiritual delirium. They stood up in his honour and chanted. The Pir waved to the clueless multitude and then gracefully adorned the ornate oversized chair. An eerie silence ensued. After a few hymns, four octogenarians came to the stage with a big unfurled turban on a golden tray. They held the ends of the cloth and stretched it across the stage. It could have been used as a sail for a small fishing boat, but was destined for a better use. Turn by turn, the octogenarians shaped it into a turban around the Pir's holy head which was still dizzy due to an overdose of the amber-coloured liquid Bachal had sent him for the occasion. Once the turban was donned, one of the octogenarians took to the dais and started enumerating the Pir's titles, interrupting these with prayers for his long life and spiritual tutelage over the sinful people of the area. After this, the Pir left the stage for the musicians to further instil spirituality into the crowd. When the first party of singers started beating their drums and playing their harmoniums, the solemn gathering turned into a religious disco. The people started swirling and swaying their heads, mostly under the effect of hashish, which gave the rhythm a quality of rushing blood. When they finished, a few musicians took turns to take the stage to play folk music. People clapped heartedly for some and booed the others off. Finally, a young boy walked confidently on to the stage and sat down in front of the microphone. He had a flute in his hand, a yellow scarf tied to his wrist. His name was announced as Murad of Deh Kamharan. Marvi saw the boy and the scarf, and her heart skipped multiple beats. Her friends whispered to her about the yellow scarf but she couldn't hear them. The boy brought the flute to his lips. The sound of the flute, mellow in its timber, filled the air. The din of the crowd ceased and absolute silence prevailed. Long, soulful, melancholic notes mesmerized the crowd with their soothing cadence. Marvi's spellbound gaze was fixed on the boy's handsome face. It was a sad song the boy was playing, foggy and faraway one moment and breaking into a warble the next. The melodious succession of tunes was rendered in rapid mutations, pouring deep into the souls of the listeners. The flautist became a part of the music he played, his body swaying gently with every rise and fall of the sound of the flute. For some mysterious reason, Marvi's eyes welled up and she buried her head in her knees.

Seven

Sitting under a thatched roof, Athee placed the kneaded clay on the wheel head and started pedalling the flywheel. As her dexterous hands continued moving, she glanced at her brother from the corner of her eye. Murad was clearly avoiding looking at her. They were in their home, which was their pottery too. The big courtyard had heaps of clay pots, pitchers and cooking pots, some damaged and others for sale. There was a kiln in the far corner and the wheel sat in the shade of the roof. Athee repeatedly cleared her throat to draw his attention, but he still refused to look at her.

'You've never played the flute like you did yesterday,' she remarked mischievously.

'Oh, really?' Murad still kept his head down, busy preparing clay.

'What came over you?' she pressed on. 'People were praising you,' she added.

'I don't care for their praise,' Murad said. He sounded glum.

'So where did you find the yellow handkerchief?' She grinned.

'I bought it,' he lied.

Athee shook her head knowingly. 'No, you didn't,' she said.

'Now you look into my eyes and tell me the truth.'

She was refusing to budge. Murad blushed and turned his head to look at her.

'I was watching when the girl gave it to you,' she revealed, and Murad had no answer.

'I didn't see you,' he said sheepishly.

'You couldn't see anything else when this was happening,' she reminded him. 'I was standing right beside her, hearing your conversation,' she laughed calmly. 'I know who she is.'

At this Murad jerked his head to look at her. He stopped kneading the clay and, after washing his hands in a bowl of water, came close to her. 'You are my sweet sister, aren't you?' He flattered her, drying his hands with the apron of his shirt.

'Of course I am. I am your mother and father too. Didn't I bring you up?' she said pleasantly.

Murad was silent for some time and then suddenly said in a sombre tone, 'I want to marry her, Athee. Isn't she pretty?'

'She sure is. But you will have to wait for a few years,' she said.

'I will, but you must see her parents and give them a proposal,' Murad said impatiently.

'I will think about it. Now get back to work. Even though in love, you will still need food to live,' she told him.

'But Athee,' Murad started in protest.

'Shush! Get back to work,' Athee waved and he reluctantly went back to his clay.

Athee was Murad's only sister, many years older to him. They had lost their parents many years ago. She had worked hard to bring him up, and there was a marvelous rapport between the two of them, brought on by love and sharing during the difficult years of their lives. Athee was a gregarious, pleasant woman with an ever-smiling face, but she had a core of steel. She was quick to laugh and hard to cry. When she was left alone to fend for herself and her three-year-old brother Murad, she decided never to marry.

'You have to promise me something,' she suddenly said in a serious voice.

Murad looked at her and was surprised to see her stern expression. 'Whatever you say,' he said earnestly.

'You will never approach her. You will do nothing to embarrass the family. They are poor but honest and honourable people,' she said while looking into his eyes.

Murad came close to her, placed his hand on her hand and softly replied, 'I promise, Athee. But please allow me to meet her once, just once. She must know I love her and she must wait for me,' he beseeched. 'After that, I will never meet her again. Not until you allow me.'

Athee glanced at his face and dewy eyes. 'Okay, just once. But no one should know about it,' she agreed.

She believed him, knowing that he never lied. He had promised and he meant it. 'Wait for a year or so and I will go to her parents. That is my promise,' she said reassuringly. 'Now get to work.'

Eight

It had been a week since the investiture ceremony and, having quenched the spiritual thirst of their souls, people had returned to the travails of life. Jannu and his compatriots had a final meeting with Comrade Haider to rejuvenate their movement against the canal. The date for the protest was finalized and messages sent to all the people at the vanguard. Jannu's impertinent son, Wali, followed the conversation keenly, quietly making his own plans. He was fed up with the ever-present calm of country life and its stale visuals. He had cherished a dream of going to the port city for years. He wanted to be part of its hustle-bustle and bathe in its dazzling light. His ears were thirsty for noise and his eyes wished to behold the sights of a busy city. After the meeting, he hitched a ride with Haider to visit a friend in another village. Some way into the journey, Haider broke the silence.

'Will you come to the city?' he asked Wali.

'I will try to if he doesn't freak out,' he said, referring to Jannu.

'You don't like it here, do you?' Haider continued.

'I hate it,' Wali was clear in his mind.

'I understand that. There is not much a young man can do

here,' Haider said. He took his business card from the dashboard and gave it to Wali. 'Keep it with you. My address and telephone number are written on it. You may need me if you reach the city.'

Wali looked at the card, and then placed it carefully in his pocket. 'I will try not to bother you,' he told Haider.

'My pleasure, Wali! Don't hesitate to ask if you need anything.'

Haider knew that he was making a good investment. Young, hot-blooded workers were what he needed in his trade.

'What do the sickle and hammer mean?' Wali asked, referring to the emblem on the card.

This was always a favourite moment for Haider. A young, gullible man asking a question in reply to which Haider could open the floodgates of doctrinal thought. As usual, he began explaining the injustices done to the poor and the need to redeem their honour and dignity. Wali, for the most part, failed to understand the intricacies of his diatribe, but became convinced that Haider was a good man. 'Snatch it if they don't give it to you' was the final message. Over the two-kilometre distance from his home to his friend's village, Haider had helped Wali redraw his roadmap for the life he planned to live. He had seeded fertile soil. When they arrived at the village, Haider stopped his Jeep and Wali jumped down. He saluted Haider, who answered the gesture with a broad smile. Then Haider shifted gear and moved on. Wali walked the rest of the distance to his friend's house and soon he was talking to Akbar, who was thrilled to see him.

'I have come to tell you to get ready for a new life.' Wali was dramatic in his manner.

'What new life, Wali?' Akbar failed to apprehend.

'We are going to the port city!' Wali revealed. 'To the city of lights, girls and money.'

'Girls in tight dresses who walk like this!' Akbar mimicked the gait of a model on a catwalk and broke into laughter. 'When?' he asked in excitement.

'They will be going to the city in a week. We will try to go with them,' Wali told him.

'Forget it. They will never allow us to join them. As usual, they will tell us that it is for elders and not for children.' Akbar sounded disappointed.

'Snatch it if they don't give it to you,' Wali said.

Akbar looked at him enquiringly. 'Your father will tell you to go catch fish and plant mangroves,' he sarcastically reminded his friend.

'I will not ask him. Trust me. We want to go, we will go,' Wali declared. 'And there is something I want you to do.'

'Tell me. Consider it done,' Akbar said.

'You will bring your father's pistol and bullets along,' Wali told him and Akbar fell silent for a few moments.

'Are you sure? What do we need the gun for?' he managed to ask hesitantly, afraid to make his friend angry.

'I am sure. But don't worry. We will not use it,' Wali assured him.

After a few pensive moments, Akbar shook his head. 'I'll do it. He doesn't carry it anyway.' They were silent for a while.

'I wish we knew someone in the city. It would have been a lot of help in finding a job,' Akbar said.

'I know someone strong and influential,' Wali said. He produced Haider's visiting card and gave it to Akbar. Unable to read the card, Akbar just sniffed it and then looked at it admiringly.

'Who is he?' he asked Wali.

'He is the same man who is leading our people in this so-called movement against the canal,' Wali replied.

'Tell me about the city,' Akbar asked in childish excitement. As

Wali tucked his hands behind his head and reclined on the grass, Akbar closed his eyes and waited for him to speak.

'I have been there only once, but I will tell you about it. It is a city where it is neither too hot nor too cold. A poor man can sleep in a park under the open sky and he will sleep peacefully. One can eat in a grand hotel if one can spend the money or eat equally delicious food sold by vendors on the roadside for a fraction of the money. The roads are wide and paved. The houses are made of bricks and cement and are a treat to look at. These don't get washed away in floods or blown away in a hurricane. There are many parks always crowded with people.' Wali paused to look at Akbar who still had his eyes closed.

'Tell me about the people,' Akbar said.

'The people have come to live in the city from every part of the country. The city is like a mother to her children. The people are educated and civilized, soft in manners and helpful in their attitude. They believe in living and letting others live. There is enough for everyone and there are no fights.'

Wali stopped talking and Akbar opened his eyes as if woken from a pleasant dream.

'We will go, Wali. I will go with you,' Akbar declared. 'But do we have to take a gun to such a wonderful place?'

'Yes, we do. We will throw it away if all goes well,' Wali insisted.

'Then so be it,' Akbar agreed.

A week later, they furtively sneaked on to the top of the bus that was taking farmers to the press club in the port city. Wali had tucked the gun Akbar had brought into the belt of his pyjamas. It felt very comforting to him. They sat silently, watching the road and waiting. After a few hours, the bus entered the outskirts of the city. When the bus stopped at a red light, they descended the staircase at the back and melded into the crowd. They were rid of all moorings at last. Or, so they thought.

~

Murad has been dreaming of Marvi ever since he met her at the investiture ceremony. Having obtained his sister's permission to meet her but once, he had hovered around the lake and Marvi's home from dawn to dusk, trying hard to avoid an encounter with the inhabitants of the area. An abandoned boat anchored near the edge of the lake closest to Marvi's home became his favourite hideout for his daily vigils. Reclining in the boat, he spent hours watching Marvi's door and hoping for her to emerge. She seldom did or did so when he was not watching. Then it happened.

It was on the day when Jannu and the other fishermen boarded the bus to the city. He saw Marvi coming out of her home, nudging a goat. His heart skipped a beat. He quickly scanned the surroundings for people and saw none. Fortunately for him, it was midday and the weather was too hot for people to leave their homes. He returned his gaze towards the thicket near her home. He jumped out of the boat and hurried in her direction. His heart was pounding. The prospect of facing her made him immensely nervous. Marvi soon disappeared in the thicket along with the goat. Step by step, he moved closer. Then he heard the goat bleating and Marvi commanding it. He hurried to reach the thicket. As he negotiated his way through the thorny bushes, his tunic got entangled. He bent down to free himself. When he raised his head, he saw Marvi standing two yards away, wide-eyed and coy, trying hard to hide her smile. They silently gazed at each other, basking in the bliss of the moment.

'Go away. Someone will see you,' Marvi finally said in a loud whisper, but her twinkling eyes belied her urging.

'I am not afraid,' Murad tried to sound confident.

'They will kill you,' she warned mockingly.

'Let them do whatever they would like to do,' he said and grasped her hand.

Feeling his warmth, she melted like wax. He pulled her closer. Head bent, she clung to him. Murad inhaled deeply to imbibe her earthy savour. The sound of Marvi's mother calling her name broke the moment and she withdrew abruptly, nervously whispering, 'Now go away.'

'Not before you make a promise,' he whispered back, still holding her wrist.

'What?' she asked.

'You will wait for me until I come to marry you,' he said, looking at her with beseeching eyes.

She blushed and lowered her gaze.

'I will. I promise,' she said, her voice heavy with emotion.

Murad released her wrist and she slowly retreated, still facing him and lovingly staring at his face.

Nine

The bus arrived at the press club where Comrade Haider was waiting for them. He had two volunteers with him who immediately distributed flags and banners among the protesters. Then they were asked to form a line and march towards the main gate of the press club. They complied, shouting their slogans. Haider was the most vehement participant in the unfolding events. Curious onlookers stopped to watch, trying to make sense of the issue. Their numbers gradually increased and spilled over onto the busy road. Jannu and his friends were surprised when they saw the spectators become agitators, shouting slogans with a zeal at par with theirs. The crowd soon became unruly and people started pelting the vehicles on the road with stones, shattering a few windshields. The trapped vehicles attempted to reverse, but the traffic behind them had come to a standstill, many of the drivers honking persistently. The adjacent roads were also becoming clogged as the crowd at the press club gate built up further. Haider jumped onto a platform and, with his eyes wide and his neck veins engorged, started making an incendiary speech, lamenting the gradual death of a land that supported thousands of poor people. Jannu noticed that the crowd of city folk was angrier than the villagers were. He and the villagers watched the interplay of disparate forces in utter confusion, but they were happy to see the uninvited supporters.

No administration could allow the mayhem to continue. Soon police trucks arrived and helmeted policemen jumped down wielding billy clubs and tear-gas guns. They blurted stern instructions over a microphone for the crowd to disperse. Then, without waiting, they charged the protesters. They were generous in the use of their clubs and tear-gas shells. The crowd retaliated by throwing the gas shells back at the police, smoke still billowing from them. The villagers didn't know what to do. Choking and coughing, they simply huddled together. The gate of the press club was quickly shut, but only after allowing Haider to enter. The fracas continued for many minutes before the crowd mysteriously disappeared into the surrounding streets. The police opened the road for traffic and vehicles started moving. It all ended as quickly as it had started, empty tear-gas shells, shoes and a few patches of blood on the road being the only remaining evidence of the unrest. But the clash had been recorded by the television news. They also covered the hurriedly arranged press conference during which Haider addressed the journalists beside Jannu and his compatriots. He explained in detail the effects of the planned outflow drain on the lives of the inhabitants of the Indus Delta and its ecology. He also invited Jannu to speak, who nervously did so in an incoherent manner. The whole package was aired on prime-time news across many channels. The villagers watched in Haider's home while having dinner. They were jubilant at this wide exposure of their misfortunes, and thanked Comrade Haider for his sagacious leadership. Jannu was still curious about the crowd of men who had championed their cause for no apparent reason. When he asked Comrade Haider, he simply smiled.

Meanwhile, Kamal Rizvi, CEO of the engineering firm that got the contract for the canal, was watching the television coverage of the event in his office, and he didn't like what he saw. He already knew well the ecological damage the canal was bound to wreak on the delta, and he also knew that the area was protected by international treaties to which his country was a signatory. The prospects of huge returns had enticed him to take a risk, believing that the illiterate and widely scattered villagers would not be able to stir a significant amount of dust to seriously threaten his project. The intrusion of this new factor, however, portended setbacks. The new factor was the man in the lead and his name was Comrade Haider. When Rizvi saw him on the TV screen, his face rang a bell somewhere in his memory. He thought hard about it but could not recall. While driving home, he decided to call a meeting of his associates and bank officials to plan their response.

Ten

Wali and Akbar felt strangely irrelevant once the bus had gone. An unfamiliar sense of emptiness engulfed them as they stood undecided on the footpath amidst a moving crowd of unfamiliar faces. There was nowhere to go now that they could go anywhere. They felt no compulsion to hurry because no one was waiting for them. There was no fear of getting lost because there was no place to return to. There were no friends but there were no enemies either. All points of reference had ceased to exist, leaving them in a place devoid of gravity.

Wali tucked the gun underneath his shirt. It now felt hard and cold, refusing to give comfort. As Akbar turned his face towards Wali, someone flicked his traditional cap off his head. With an angry shout, he turned to get hold of the person but could not decide whom to grab. He picked up his cap and, muttering profanities, dusted it. He then placed it back on his head with a forward tilt, so it appeared menacing, and looked at Wali who was also seething with anger at this disrespect. They started walking forward aimlessly, trying to become part of the whole.

'Let us eat something. I am hungry,' Wali said.

'We have to be careful with our money. We don't have much,' Akbar reminded him.

'But we have to eat,' Wali said, and dragged him into a crowded restaurant. 'This must be cheap. I can see only labourers.'

They found an empty table and sat down. It was a noisy place. The dishevelled waiters were scurrying around with plates and bread to serve to the customers. Every now and then, a bell rang loudly and a man behind the cash counter blurted out instructions.

'Hit number nine with two plates of rice.'

'Thirty rupees from number three.'

'Number two has been waiting for a long time. Hit them with two plates of chicken gravy and four pieces of bread.'

Wali figured out that the man was referring to table numbers and that by 'hit' he meant 'serve'. They watched the activity in amazement.

'Okay?' someone said, and they turned to find a boy of their age standing by the table. He was one of the waiters.

'Two cups of tea and biscuits,' Wali said.

The boy went and soon returned with their order.

'What is your name?' Akbar asked the boy.

'Why do you ask?' the boy replied curtly.

'You look familiar,' Wali lied.

'Are you from the interior?' the boy asked, lowering his voice. By 'interior' he meant the rural areas of the province.

'Yes, we are,' Wali replied, taking a bite of a biscuit.

The boy smiled at this. 'I am Pannu. I am from Tando Adam. Welcome to the jungle,' he said dramatically.

They shook hands and Pannu was about to say something more when the man behind the cash counter shouted, 'Hurry up, boy. Don't waste time.'

'I will be back,' Pannu said quickly and got back to work.

He returned after fifteen minutes. They left the restaurant and found a place on the footpath to sit and smoke a cigarette. There, they introduced themselves to each other in greater detail. Wali told him that he had come to find work in the city and that they had no place to stay and very little money. Pannu offered to share his room with them until they found a job. Both of them agreed gladly. Akbar credited Pir Muazzam Shah's spiritual powers for this rare bit of luck. For Wali, it was serendipity.

Eleven

Night came to the lake, and with it an eerie silence occasionally interrupted by barking dogs. Nooran and Marvi felt insecure in the absence of both men in the house. They harkened to every mysterious sound and heard imaginary footsteps approaching the bush house. Jannu had never left his family alone, especially not at night, out of fear of marauding gangs of dacoits. They weren't expecting him to return before the next day, but Wali should have been there and there was no sign of him either. Nooran ate her dinner early and retired to her bed to seek refuge in the oblivion of sleep. Marvi heard her heavy breathing and periodic snoring and braced herself for a lonely night. She was scared, but also worried for Wali. She had heard many stories about dacoits venturing out during the night in search of late travellers and unprotected women. She also believed in ghosts and evil spirits and was imagining them lurking in the dark corners. With her mother in the realm of the semi-dead, she was left alone to fend for herself. She sat near the hearth for a long time, scratching the ash and thinking about her brother. She prayed for his safety. Time had ceased to flow and total silence was beginning to haunt her.

Then she heard it. Riding a gentle breeze, the sound of the flute reached her ears. She smiled softly. 'It must be him,' she said to herself. She felt her anxiety leave her. There was someone out there thinking of her. She was not alone. Murad's face materialized out of the darkness and, in her mind, he came and sat beside her, lovingly looking at her and smiling. A soft patch of light fell on her monochromatic world, like a feather falling on still water without creating ripples. The light split into all the colours of the rainbow and flooded her soul.

'Go away,' she murmured, but the face of the flautist remained. She closed her eyes and lent her ears to the sound of the flute. Love had conquered fear. She lay on her bed, looking at the stars until sleep overtook her.

～

Around the same time, Wali opened his eyes in Pannu's room. It was the ruffle of Pannu leaving his bed that had awoken him. Lying still and feigning sleep, he saw Pannu kneeling over Akbar and then over him as if to ascertain whether they were asleep or awake. He then tiptoed to his cupboard and slowly opened it. Wali heard a lock click open and a drawer being pulled out. Wali turned his head and saw him take out a packet from the drawer. In the dim light of a bulb in the corridor, Wali saw Pannu take out a stack of notes and count them. He then wrapped them back up and carefully placed them in the drawer. He didn't forget to lock the drawer before returning to bed. 'He had been carelessly careful,' Wali thought and smiled at his oxymoron.

They woke early the next morning and took turns cleaning up in the bathroom. Pannu brought them breakfast with hot tea.

'You should not have taken the trouble,' Akbar said, impressed by his gesture of hospitality.

'You know that it is in our tradition to take care of guests,' Pannu replied.

They ate sitting in a circle on the floor.

Halfway through the meal, Pannu asked, 'So what are your plans for the day?'

'We will see. Maybe we will go and look for a job,' Akbar replied.

'Can I give you some advice?' Pannu asked.

'Sure,' Akbar said.

'Don't wear your traditional caps when you go out,' he said.

'Why?' both Akbar and Wali asked together, surprised at his advice.

'This is what our forefathers wore. We take pride in our traditional dress,' Wali protested.

'You are welcome to take pride in it; I do as well. But there is no point in making a statement of it,' Pannu advised them. 'It is a feral city you have come to, simmering with hatred. The city has been flooded with firearms since the Afghan war. Society has fragmented like never before. People live among their own and prefer to remain that way.'

As Pannu spoke, Akbar looked at Wali with a sense of confused betrayal. This did not sound like the peaceful city that had been described to him.

'As for your jobs, let me speak to some people I know. No one gives a job to a stranger these days,' Pannu added.

Akbar thought for a moment and then nodded. 'We will do that, Pannu, and thank you very much.'

'You can roam about the city while I am at work. I will give you the spare key to the room so you can come back when you are tired.' He got up to leave. Before stepping out, he handed the spare key to Wali.

A few minutes after Pannu left, Wali asked Akbar to bring him a packet of cigarettes. Akbar was too glad to oblige him. Wali shut and bolted the door after he was gone. He went to the cupboard and examined the cheap lock. It was not difficult to break open. He pulled the drawer out and found the money Pannu had stashed inside. He counted the crisp notes; there were around thirty thousand rupees. He tucked the money into a secret pocket of his shirt. When Akbar returned, Wali was ready to go.

'Are we leaving?' Akbar asked, handing him the cigarettes in surprise.

'Yes, we are. Take all your things. We'll not be coming back.'

Twelve

When Jannu returned home, Wali was not with him as Nooran and Marvi had expected.

'Where is Wali?' she asked her husband, scanning the dirt road with restless eyes.

'How would I know?' Jannu asked impatiently. 'He didn't accompany us.'

'He is not at home. We have not seen him since you left,' she said anxiously.

'Stop panicking. He must be with his friends,' Jannu consoled her.

'He always returns home for the night. This has never happened before!' she exclaimed in protest.

Jannu felt his euphoria from the successful campaign at the press club drain away. The possibility of losing his only son started sinking in and, as it did, his frustration was growing. He became angry.

'If he is gone, he is gone. What can I do?' He sat down helplessly on a cot, holding his head in his hands.

Marvi was watching her parents; seeing her father giving up hope, she could not hold back her tears. She started wailing.

'Don't add to our worries. Just shut up,' her mother rebuked her.

Jannu abruptly stood up. 'Let us go and look for him.'

Soon, the three of them were briskly walking toward the lake where Jannu's boat was anchored. They went from village to village and from door to door. They walked, rowed and hitchhiked on donkey carts in search of Wali. People listened to them in sympathy and shared their anxiety, suggested where to look for their lost son and offered them food and water, but no one knew Wali's whereabouts. They threw compassionate glances at the frail Nooran, whose eyes were restless to see her son, and commiserated with her for the loss. Their relatives and friends expressed optimism that the boy would return in a few days, but they didn't believe their own words. Whosoever knew Wali knew that the roguish young man was gone for good. So did Jannu and Nooran. After all, they were his parents. Nevertheless, they didn't hesitate to walk the extra mile in their futile search.

It was late in the night when the bow of their boat hit the shore on the return journey. They scurried toward their bush house in the hope of seeing a lamp burning or the door unlocked, but the house was shrouded in darkness and the door was still bolted. Their last hope left them like a bird flying away suddenly and silently, the same way their son had gone.

~

The callow boys from the far-flung village of fishermen were loving the smog and chaos of the city. They walked aimlessly on the footpath, stopping to observe the mannequins in shop windows. The huge billboards with pictures of pretty women fascinated them. They chased any women they saw, but preferred fashionable ones with painted lips and sunglasses. At times, their manner was so rude that the shopkeepers had to shoo them away. Their tilted caps and swagger provoked passers-by to look at them with dislike. They didn't fail to notice this dislike and were increasingly irked. Wali was itching to pick a fight, but Akbar kept dragging him away. When Wali brushed against a woman who was bargaining with a vendor, she furiously turned and screamed at them.

'Keep your distance,' she said, and then added, 'Animals.'

Wali was infuriated at this insult. He was about to retaliate, but noticed some men were ready to respond if he dared. They sheepishly hurried away, their heads hanging low.

'Back home I would have killed her,' Wali said, grinding his teeth.

'We should know that this is different turf,' Akbar reminded him. 'Let us have a cold drink to cool you down.'

Akbar held his hand as they walked along the footpath. The midday sun was hot, the air humid and filled with smoke, and both of them were sweating profusely. The cacophony of the busy bazaar was unremitting. A cold drink vendor had set up his shop on the footpath and placed a row of chairs for his clients to sit as if at a restaurant. They took two bottles of soft drink and began to relish the sweet soda.

'It was a mistake to leave Pannu's place,' Akbar said.

'We had to,' Wali replied.

'Why?' Akbar asked.

'Because I stole his money,' Wali said.

'You stole his money?! How much?' Akbar could not believe his ears.

'Thirty thousand rupees,' Wali replied.

'You stole money from that nice man?! Why?' Akbar raised his voice.

'Because one cannot steal from a nasty man,' Wali said sardonically.

Astounded, Akbar looked at him for a few moments and then broke into a loud laughter. 'You son of a bitch. You son of a bitch. How could you do such a thing?'

He kept laughing and Wali joined him. Suddenly, they saw a car screech to a stop just a few feet away. Two boys stormed out of the car carrying guns, and within seconds, sprayed the man sitting three chairs away with bullets. As his lifeless body slumped to the footpath, one of the boys walked up to him and shot him once more in the head at close range. The boys watched the drama in a daze, paralyzed with fear. The killers walked back to the car with terrible aplomb and the car drove away. Within seconds, the road was left deserted and a sepulchral silence prevailed.

Wali turned his face towards Akbar and could hardly mutter, 'Run, Akbar. Let us go before the police arrive. I have the gun tucked in my belt.'

They managed to get up and stagger away as quickly as they could.

Thirteen

The atmosphere in the boardroom was foreboding. A group of sullen bankers shared the table with Rizvi and his equally sullen associates. Also present were a few unruffled government officials with their hair and moustaches dyed jet black and gaudy ties around their necks. Apart from the bankers, the rest were beneficiaries of the lucrative project of the outfall drain.

'The ecology of the wetlands has remained of grave concern to the bank from the start. You promised to take this factor into consideration while planning the project,' a piqued bank official said when the participants had settled.

'The planning and design was the responsibility of the government,' one of Rizvi's associates said in defence.

'So we did,' a government official declared confidently. 'There are no flaws in the design.'

The bankers exchanged sarcastic smiles and then one of them said, 'The man answering questions in the press conference was well prepared. He said something about the tidal link and the direction in which the water is going to flow. It made a lot of sense.'

The government officials were at a loss for words, so Rizvi

came to their defence.

'I didn't see the whole press conference but I assure you, this man is a rabble-rouser trying to raise a storm in a cup of tea,' he said.

'We are more concerned with what the indigenous people came to say than we are with rabble-rousers.' The banker was beginning to lose patience. 'May I remind you that the outfall drain is not just a canal passing through arid lands? It is a canal which will bring a lot of stuff to a region which is a Ramsar Site and is protected by international treaties, to which your country is a signatory,' he added in an angry tone.

'Our technical experts have been asked to reassess the design submitted to us. Until a decision is reached, we will have to delay the release of funds,' another banker joined in.

Rizvi didn't like what he was hearing. 'Please, please. Don't reach hurried conclusions. The segment that is under objection has not been reached as yet. Let the work continue and let your experts revisit the design. It will be the end of the project if funds were delayed. I have already invested millions into it,' he pleaded.

'We will consider your concerns, but we don't promise anything if these protests continue. We attach great importance to the lives of common men and their habitats. Please remember that,' the banker announced.

The parlay continued for a couple more hours. By the end of the discussion, Rizvi was convinced of the serious nature of the threat he was facing. When the sour bankers and clueless government officials left the conference room, Rizvi was left alone with his beneficiaries. They expressed their apprehensions openly once the outsiders had gone. Rizvi heard them patiently.

'They are right. The wetlands are a protected region and our country is a signatory to all the international conventions. This fact would have gone unnoticed had it not been for the few who raised awareness amongst the people of the delta region. Still, their protests would have remained insignificant if this Comrade Haider had not intervened,' one of his colleagues said.

'How could we have missed this gathering storm?' another colleague wondered.

'I knew about the unrest, but my assessment was that logistically it was difficult for the widely scattered people without means to be able to make any difference. But I agree that the intrusion of this man may change the game,' Rizvi said. 'Now I will ask my engineers to come up with a solution to the flaws that have surfaced. Meanwhile, I would like to meet Comrade Haider and read his mind.'

Fourteen

After Wali's disappearance, the responsibility of helping Jannu in his fishing trips fell on Marvi's shoulders. Her mother, for some unexplained reason, blamed her for Wali going away and leaving them alone, although the loss had taken its toll on her as well and she had been grieving ever since. She was having a miserable time. It appeared to her as if her happy days had left her for good and sadness had settled in her soul. She was quick to cry and lash out angrily at her mother, whose baleful gaze never left her. She wanted to scream and tear away from the sadness but instead dissembled and cocooned herself in an imaginary world where few people could intrude. While shepherding her goats in the thicket near her home, she would sit in the shade of a bush and wander away into a fairyland where someone played his flute for her and hid behind dense foliage and flowers on the vine. She would try to find him, chasing him for a while and then sitting to sulk angrily. He would always sneak up from behind and whisper in her ear, which would make her blush. They would frolic together until they slumped exhausted on luxurious grass. To her dismay, she always returned to harsh realities at the sound of her bleating goats.

The chance of accompanying her father in his work was an opportunity to stay away from her carping mother and her internal upheavals. She was no stranger to the work. She knew how to prepare the net for casting and had learned how to retrieve it. She was adept at mending it too and could stitch tears in the two sails of the boat her father owned.

On the second day that the daughter and father returned from the hunt, they saw a gleaming red tractor and its trolley parked near the house. An important-looking man was reclining against the cushion on their cot and talking to a person sitting nearby on a stool. They stopped at some distance to take stock of the situation.

'Whoever it is, he is an important man,' Jannu said, and darted forward with Marvi scrambling in his footsteps.

'Welcome, welcome to this poor man's home,' Jannu shouted, spreading his arms open in a gesture of salutation.

Bachal obliged him by extending his right hand for him to kiss and shake, while ogling Marvi from head to toe. His stare was so intense that Marvi felt a shiver run down her spine, and she lowered her thick eyelashes. Bachal relished the moment.

'This is my master Bachal,' Mithal announced with panache. 'We will spend the night here. Make sure the landlord is comfortable. He has brought some goods for you. Take these from the trolley and prepare a meal worthy of his highness.'

Mithal waved for Jannu to follow him. Both of them walked towards the tractor.

'What is your name?' Bachal asked Marvi when they had gone.

'Marvi.' She could hardly whisper.

'That is a lovely name.' He revealed his teeth with receding gums. 'Go and help your father,' he said, and, as Marvi immediately obeyed, he turned to admire her swaying hips, which held his interest until she reached the tractor.

Bachal had brought grains, sugar, spices, cooking oil and cutlery for them. Nooran placed the goods in the corner of her room, profusely praising Bachal's generosity all the while. She was obliged to have this honourable man as their guest. Marvi was asked to light a fire in two hearths, and Nooran started cooking the rice and cereals Bachal had brought with the utensils he had donated to them. The family contributed freshly caught fish to the meal, and Marvi and Jannu had to keep shuttling in and out of the house in the service of Bachal. Nooran had initially expressed slight reservation in sending Marvi out alone, but Jannu dismissed her concerns.

'He is an old man, the age of her grandfather if he were alive,' he said.

But he was already finding it hard to maintain his dignity in servitude. To Bachal's dismay, daylight rapidly receded to give way to darkness. Two lanterns were lit and he realized that Marvi looked more beautiful in the light of the flames.

Dinner was served and both Bachal and Mithal ate to their hearts' delight, praising the culinary expertise of Nooran, who squatted nearby on the ground like a worshipper in front of an idol. After dinner, a bed was prepared for Bachal in the tractor trolley and a mosquito net hoisted over it like a canopy. Mithal decided to sleep on the cot after dragging it closer to the tractor, in case his master needed him. Bachal stretched out on his bed after the meal, thinking of Marvi. Mithal had been right in his description of the girl. He imagined a life in her company, Marvi sitting with him in his favourite swing chair and chirping like a bird.

'Mithal,' he called loudly, and in no time Mithal was peeping into the trolley.

'Yes, master?' he asked.

'How did you know about her?' Bachal inquired.

'From the people, master. She is mentioned often in conversation,' Mithal replied.

'Hmm. Mithal, she is like a flower in danger of wilting away in poverty. She should be in a castle.' Bachal smiled.

'That is why we are here, master,' Mithal said and grinned, showing his yellow teeth. 'But we will have to wait,' he added.

'Do you think her parents will agree to my proposal?' Bachal asked. He had been feeling his age since he had seen her.

'One word from Pir Muazzam Shah and they will consider it their divine duty to comply,' Mithal said.

After a few moments of silence, Bachal shook his head. 'No. I will not involve him in this affair. He is a malicious man and can have selfish thoughts,' he said. 'I would not like to force her. I want to win her over.'

'You will succeed, master. I am sure you will,' Mithal prophesied.

Then the sound of a flute reached their ears. It appeared to come from far away in the direction of the lake. They fell silent and harkened to the mesmerizing tune.

'What time is it, Mithal?' Bachal asked.

'Almost midnight, master,' Mithal whispered back.

'Who is this flautist and why has he come to this wilderness in the middle of the night to play a flute. Is it a serenade?' Bachal wondered aloud.

'That is a question that needs to be answered,' Mithal said in a worried tone. 'Go to sleep, master. Leave the worries to me.'

This comforted Bachal, who turned in his bed and closed his eyes. But the sound of the flute haunted Mithal for a long time before he dozed off.

Fifteen

The boys spent their second night on the bare floor of a shrine's crowded guest house. It was again a restless night. They ate with the other urchins from the food brought by devotees and spent the day looking at people who came to the shrine to pay respects. This atmosphere was not alien to them, as they had similar shrines of holy men in their area as well. But they knew they could not continue this way of life. They had come looking for higher standards. The brazen murder that they had witnessed had terrorized them, and, to their chagrin, they had realized that the world was a tougher place to live than they had imagined, and that they were not as brave as they had fancied themselves. Both of them had individually replayed the scene of the bloodied body slumping on to the road and decided to tread more softly on the ground. With their hubris evaporating into thin air, they were in a position to make realistic decisions.

'I think we should seek help from Comrade Haider,' Wali said to Akbar.

'We should have done that the day we arrived,' Akbar agreed.

They walked out of the shrine and headed towards a waiting

rickshaw. They showed the driver Haider's visiting card and squeezed into the rickshaw once the driver had agreed to take them. Two hours later, they were sitting with Haider at his house. Comrade Haider welcomed them warmly and heard their story with full attention. Then, he spoke to them like a sympathetic elder.

'I want you to know that the city you have come to is a jungle. It has changed over the past few years. Many different ethnic groups are claiming their right to ownership in this sprawling home of millions, and, in the process, they have turned against each other. A few years ago, no one carried even a small knife, but now, firearms are owned by everyone, thanks to national and international conspirators. You will never know whether the man next to you is a friend or a foe,' he explained.

'But Wali told me it was a civilized city of educated people! That is why I came,' Akbar said, disappointed at these revelations.

'I can only laugh at that,' Haider snickered. 'Shake off any illusions now that you have decided to live here. And start taking care of yourselves. The poor love to fleece the poor. They have been let loose on each other so the puppetmasters are left alone. Puppetmasters across all types of divides! But you will not understand such things. I can find you jobs but on one condition,' he said, and then waited for their response.

'What condition, sir?' Wali asked after a few moments.

'You will work for me when I need you,' Haider told them.

'What type of work?' Akbar was inquisitive.

'That, you will be told when the opportunity arises. But don't worry, you will be paid well,' he reassured them.

The boys looked at each other in confusion but had no alternative except to agree.

'My servant will share his room with you until I find jobs for you. Until then, be careful. Don't wear your caps when you go out.'

The next day the boys were given the address of a garage and told to report to a man called Mistry Afzal. They again took a rickshaw and reached the address. It was a wide compound with a few cars and six apprentices busy with work.

'Are you sure you want to work here?' Mistry called from under a car he was busy fixing.

'That is why we have come,' Wali replied.

The euphoria of finding jobs had blunted the sharpness of the horrible event they had witnessed there the day before, and the boys were regaining their confidence. Ironically, the more they thought and talked about the murder, the less they were afraid. They were becoming acclimatized to the incident.

Mistry dragged himself out and stood up. He looked at them from head to toe. They looked raw and obtuse. He felt pity for them and asked them to follow him to his office—a small cluttered room in a corner of the compound. He told them about their wages and the nature of their work.

'You will assist my boys in their work. Do as you are told. Keep your eyes open and try to learn. It may do you good in the future. Now, come and let me introduce you to the boys.' He rose from his chair but said one final thing before stepping out. 'No fights! One fight and you are out. Is that understood?' He looked at them.

'Absolutely,' Wali said.

Sixteen

With seagulls squawking above, the boat skimmed over the still waters of the lake in the gentle breeze of dawn. Jannu had tried his best to make his boat comfortable for his important guest, who was reclining over a cushion, his eyes roving from the seagulls to Marvi and back. Marvi was sitting three yards away and preparing the net for casting. Bachal had his twelve-bore shotgun in his lap, loaded, with the safety catch turned off. Mithal was scanning the lake and the sky for geese. The morning breeze, twilight of dawn and presence of Marvi had filled Bachal with amorous thoughts. Every once in a while, she would sneak a look at his rifle and quiver at the thought of seeing a bloodied goose in agony, slapping the surface of the water with its wings. Bachal sensed her fear and smiled in amusement.

'Mithal, I don't see any geese and my hands are itching,' he said meaningfully to his servant.

'In that case why don't you shoot down the seagulls? They are very noisy,' Mithal replied.

Bachal lifted his rifle, secured the butt against his right shoulder and feigned aiming at the seagulls. Marvi looked at him in horror and tightly squeezed her eyes shut in apprehension, expecting the sound of the gun. Bachal's gun was pointed towards the seagulls, but his eyes were on Marvi and he was smiling in amusement. Mithal and Jannu were also enjoying the charade. After a while, when she didn't hear a shot, she opened her eyes and saw the three men looking at her. She blushed in embarrassment and covered her face with both her hands. Bachal was destroyed.

He walked up to her, and sat near her. He said, 'You are such a timid young lady.' His voice was heavy with feeling. 'You don't like my gun?' he asked.

'No, I don't,' she muttered.

'Then to hell with it,' he said briefly, and threw the rifle into the water.

Mithal could only scream at this waste of a precious weapon. 'Master!'

Jannu and Marvi were also dumbfounded, but Bachal was simply smiling.

'Happy?' he asked Marvi.

Marvi was too shocked to reply.

'If *you* don't like it, *I* don't like it,' he said to Marvi.

Jannu was puzzled at his gesture. He didn't know how to react, but attributed the act to the riches and kind heart of an old man. Silence prevailed for some time, each trying to recover from the jolt.

'Did you hear the flute last night?' Bachal broke the silence, addressing Jannu.

Marvi's heart skipped a beat.

'Flute? No, I didn't. I was fast asleep,' Jannu replied.

'I wonder who was playing it, in the middle of the night in this wilderness,' Bachal continued. 'He was probably here on the lake, sitting in one of the boats.'

'Yes, you must be right. I have heard others talking about it. They say he always plays the same tune,' Jannu replied.

'It was an alluring sound,' Bachal said, all this time looking at Marvi for any change of expression. He encountered innocent detachment.

'There is no dearth of mad people here,' Jannu said, bending to pick up the net.

He cinched the free line tightly to his left wrist, then loosely coiled it into a few loops. Taking the horn of the net in his left hand, he split the rest of the net in half with his right hand and threw the lower half over his left shoulder. He twisted his body at the waist and, unleashing the coils, threw the net over the water. The net fanned out as he released it and sank into the water. After some time, he deftly hauled it back and Marvi screamed with excitement when she saw a few fishes with simmering white bellies tossing and turning, trying to set themselves free. They disentangled the fish and filled their icebox with their catch. Mithal and Bachal saw all this, and admired his expertise.

'That was good work, Jannu,' Bachal said, coming over to examine the catch.

'Master, if your method is right, you will catch the fish,' Mithal said and Bachal smiled at his veiled analogy.

They stayed at the lake until the sun had travelled across half the sky. All this time, Jannu kept busy with his fishing and Marvi continued helping.

'You need a new boat,' Bachal called to Jannu.

'Boats are expensive, sir,' Jannu responded.

'With friends like him, nothing is expensive for you,' Mithal quipped.

'Of course, of course,' Bachal was flattered. 'Just say the word, Jannu,' he said.

'You are very generous, sir,' Jannu felt obliged and said, 'I am honoured to have you as a friend.'

'You haven't seen his generosity yet,' Mithal remarked, and they laughed.

Bachal asked Jannu to head to shore, as he wanted to leave early. Jannu adjusted his sail and the boat changed its direction. When they reached Jannu's house, he placed the icebox in the trolley for Bachal to take with him. Bachal rewarded him amply by giving a few crisp five-hundred rupee notes to Nooran. They promised to come back soon and said their goodbyes. Then Bachal climbed into the driver's seat and was seen off by the family, waving gratefully.

Bachal drove in silence for quite some time. He rarely spoke to Mithal except during their evening sessions of drinking together. Mithal understood the meaning of his silence. He knew he was thinking of Marvi.

'You will have to wait for a couple of years,' Mithal said to break the silence, and Bachal reacted as if woken from a dream.

'I know,' he murmured back, knowing that Mithal was referring to Marvi's age.

'I suggest you not throw away this opportunity like Jannu tossed back the fingerlings. He could have kept them in a pond and they would have grown,' Mithal said.

'Hmm,' Bachal remained preoccupied by his thoughts. They kept silent for another few miles.

Then Bachal saw four men some distance away from the dirt road. He stopped the tractor and asked Mithal to call them over. Mithal went running to them and the men, after some hesitation, accompanied him back. They wore jeans and were carrying land survey equipment.

'Are you land surveyors?' Bachal asked.

'Yes we are,' one of them said.

'What are you doing in this wilderness?' Bachal asked.

'We are charting a course for the canal,' they replied.

'The canal? Oh, I see.' Bachal knew of the turmoil the project had created. 'So it is for real?'

'It is, sir,' one of them replied. 'It is a government undertaking.'

'I heard there is a lot of acrimony among the local people,' Bachal said. 'Have you faced any hostility?'

'Of course. We are thinking of bringing a police guard next time,' the men told him.

Bachal was silent for a moment before asking in a serious tone, 'Is it going to be very harmful to this area?'

The man thought for a long moment and then disappointed Bachal with a simple reply. 'To be frank, we don't know. We are only trying to earn our living.'

'Of course, of course,' Bachal laughed heartily. 'Only a few know while the rest just make a living. You remind me of soldiers in war. No one has a clue why they are fighting.' He shifted gear and the tractor moved on. 'Take care, my friends,' he shouted over the noise of the engine.

Seventeen

The more Rizvi thought about it, the more ominous it looked. He had ordered work to continue on the canal, but the banks had stopped releasing funds until the issue was hashed out to the satisfaction of their experts and the inhabitants of the wetlands. The final stretch of the canal was his predicament. The flow of water in the tidal link was against the natural gradient of flow, and there was only one solution to this problem—an impossible one. The canal had to course through the neighbouring country across the border if the gradient was to be followed. In the present design, seawater was bound to backflow during high tide, causing the toxic water of the canal to spill over onto land in a wide area. Rizvi had asked his engineers to find an alternate solution, but working in the area was becoming increasingly hazardous. His teams had been repeatedly attacked and their equipment broken. His engineers were reluctant to go into the field. He had been advised not to risk further investment in the project but had turned down the suggestion. He was told that Comrade Haider was working with the activists and planning a convention of farmers and politicians to force the government to abandon the project. He was familiar with the politicians who had been invited. They were the type of people who resisted construction of any type; no matter what it was. He was leery of their intentions and knew that if they joined the fray, he would be forced to give up. It was in this frame of mind that he decided to meet Comrade Haider. He asked his manager to invite him for talks.

Because of the sunglasses and the thick moustache and beard that covered most of Comrade Haider's face, Rizvi's manager failed to read his expression when he met him to offer the invitation. However, the man agreed to see his boss. A date and time were fixed and the manager left in confusion regarding Comrade Haider's feelings about the meeting.

On the appointed day, Haider walked into Rizvi's office, clad in his trademark hand-loomed clothes, looking earnest and sombre. Rizvi warmly shook his hand and thanked him profusely for coming. Comrade Haider was more restrained in the exchange of pleasantries, but he did reciprocate with nice words. After a round of nostalgic talk about the honest politics of yore, Rizvi tactfully brought up the subject of the canal. He attempted to touch Comrade Haider's supposed tender points.

'I was a bit surprised at your stand because I know about your lifelong struggle in the cause of the poor. This canal will render vast swathes of land in upper areas suitable for cultivation once more. Thousands of peasants will be able to earn a living once again, send their children to school and get their daughters married. When they told me of a prominent politician with a glorious past opposing the project, I didn't believe it.'

Rizvi paused and was surprised to see Comrade Haider bursting into a loud laughter. He laughed for a while and Rizvi could not help but notice the cavities left by extracted premolars in his mouth. He didn't understand the joke.

'Prominent politician with a glorious past!' Haider repeated, making a visible effort to control his laughter. 'I think you should have believed it.'

'I was only paying you a compliment, sir,' Rizvi uttered meekly.

'Thank you, but I find your statement ironic. The glorious past has led to a difficult present,' he said in a matter-of-fact manner. 'Let us come to the subject of the outfall drain.'

'Yes,' Rizvi rushed. 'I have arranged a presentation for you. I would appreciate it if you saw it first, while you have your coffee.'

Rizvi invited him to an adjacent conference room. Haider nodded his head and accompanied him. While Haider was handed a cup of coffee with biscuits, an assistant of Rizvi's started flashing slides on a screen, simultaneously explaining the benefits of the canal on the waterlogged lands it was to traverse. Then he came to the final course and its descent into the sea.

'That is where you are wrong.' Haider raised his hand and interrupted the presentation. 'It will not descend into the sea. It will rather "ascend" into the sea.'

The presenter stopped short and looked helplessly at Rizvi.

'Okay. So your main objections pertain to the final segment,' Rizvi asked.

'Yes, and a few more,' Haider replied.

'Can we continue our discussion in the office?' Rizvi asked.

'Sure.' Haider got up from his chair.

Once in the office, Rizvi waited for his assistant to leave. 'So you object to the design of the link canal?'

'Mainly,' Haider replied briefly.

'If we, you and I, reach an agreement on this segment, do you guarantee that the people of this area will back off?' he asked.

Haider was silent for a while, assessing his hand of cards. 'There is a solution for every problem,' he finally said, preferring to remain vague.

'Would you agree to work with me to find a solution to this problem?' Rizvi asked.

'I may,' Haider chose to remain obscure.

Rizvi understood his vagueness. He took a step forward, his hand extended. Haider also stood up and clasped his hand. It was a long, warm handshake. The atmosphere lost its hostility and more coffee was served along with the finest confectionary the city could offer. They were joined by a pair of Rizvi's associates and their discussion veered towards the conference Haider and the leaders of the movement were planning.

'It will balloon the problem,' one of Rizvi's associates said apprehensively.

'That is exactly the aim,' Haider grinned back.

'I am afraid the problem will slip out of our hands,' Rizvi said.

'I have been at the helm of affairs so far and I will make sure that only the right decisions are made,' Haider said, and rose to leave.

Rizvi accompanied him to the car park to see him off. While shaking hands, Rizvi said, 'It is satisfying to know that you are at the helm, but I hear firebrand politicians of different shades and colours have also been invited. They may make the going rough for you.' He anxiously waited for a reply.

'They are a bunch of puerile lads. No one is going to make the going rough for me,' Haider said calmly. 'Thank you, Rizvi,' he added as the other man opened the door of his jeep for him. 'You are a kind and considerate man.'

'Just wait and see.' Rizvi smiled, and closed the door.

'Join us in the conference. You must,' Haider said.

'Do you really mean it?' Rizvi asked.

'I mean it. Consider this an official invitation. I am going to invite your bankers and government officials too. Are you interested?' he asked.

'Sure, why not,' Rizvi accepted.

'I am expecting a very large attendance from the inhabitants of the delta. After all, they are the people who will stand to win or lose,' Haider said.

'I hope I don't become the one to lose,' Rizvi said in a worried tone.

'Trust your friend.' Haider grinned good-heartedly and turned the ignition key.

Eighteen

Mistry Afzal's garage was located in a busy bazaar in an overly populated area. A big black gate opened onto a fairly large courtyard surrounded by a boundary wall. There were two small rooms in a corner and two bathrooms for the employees. In another corner, a makeshift shed had been erected. The courtyard was occupied by cars brought in for repairs. There were two teams of workers, one specialized in bodywork and the other in handling engine faults. It was quite a busy place because Mistry had earned a good reputation over the twenty-five years since he opened the garage.

Mistry was a kind but serious man in his late fifties. He took interest in teaching the young boys who came to work with him and was respected by them. Wali and Akbar were allowed to sleep in the garage until they could find a place of their own. Occasionally, other boys also spent the night in the garage if they had worked late or there was unrest in the city and it was risky to go home. Two senior apprentices had taken up most of Mistry Afzal's work, leading the two teams of workers. He placed a lot of trust in them.

The work in the garage proved to be interesting. Both Akbar and Wali were asked to assist the mechanical team and strictly advised to carry out orders. Soon, their leader impressed them with his expertise as they watched him remove faults in engines and the vehicles roar back to life at the turn of ignition keys. They carried out his orders with alacrity, hoping to grow in his image in due time. They started working with zeal, screwing and unscrewing jammed nuts and bolts and washing them in petrol. It proved to be a good start and a week passed.

The other boys were like any other bunch of raw youth. They worked, made jokes and laughed. Somehow, Wali and Akbar were finding it hard to assimilate. The callow villagers could not speak their language very well and often made silly mistakes. They first became targets of their disparaging jokes when they had to be shown how to flush the toilet. They had feigned amusement but were embittered in reality. Their naiveté and the resultant mockery by their co-workers were beginning to irritate them. They complained to Mistry Afzal, who listened to them patiently.

'I can appreciate your feelings,' he said, 'but I will advise you to ignore them. Let them behave as they want to. Concentrate on your work. I don't know why you chose to leave your homes and come to this city, but now that you have come, play safe. You have no idea how cruel people can be.'

Then he reassured them that he would talk to the others and stop them from poking fun at Akbar and Wali. They returned dissatisfied.

One of their co-workers was a charming young boy of fair complexion. Akbar took particular offence when he also snickered and tittered when the others were poking fun at them. Akbar had developed a liking for him since his arrival and the boy often returned his fixed stare with a smile.

One day, Mistry Afzal rang in the morning to ask them to keep the gate shut and for anyone who had arrived for work to go back home. He informed them that a strike had been called in the city, and there was fear of violence against any vehicles venturing out onto the roads. The foreman who received the call asked the boys to leave. Everyone left except the charming young lad, whose home was far away. One of his friends agreed to stay back with him to give him company. The foreman also left, asking Wali to close the gate and remain inside. Forces now reduced to two against two, the charming lad and his friend chose to be more prudent and avoid cracking jokes that would agitate Wali and Akbar. The four of them sat down to play cards; the charming lad teaching Akbar how to play. Akbar was thoroughly enjoying his company and missed no opportunity to rub against him and shake his hand. Wali made tea for all of them and they chatted, sipping the tea. He was glad at this evolving friendship. Suddenly, the noise of a commotion distracted them, and they ran towards the gate to see what it was.

They saw a gang of protestors pelting stones at a rickshaw and the rickshaw overturning as it veered out of their way. The crowd dragged the driver out and beat him with sticks until he was unconscious. Then, they set the rickshaw on fire and flames leapt towards the sky. The sound of a screaming siren rose at some distance and the crowd melted away into side streets within seconds, leaving the road deserted. Wali returned to his place, aghast at the ruthlessness of the crowd and the electrifying pace of events. They all sat silently, watching black smoke billowing towards the sky from places near and afar. The eerie silence that had engulfed the city was repeatedly broken by volleys of gunfire and wailing sirens. It seemed as if Lucifer had descended upon the city with a slew of companions to have a field day. At noon, Mistry Afzal called again, asking whether everything was alright. Wali told him of the event that had occurred on the road.

'Keep the gate shut. Don't go out. There are violent riots everywhere and many people have been killed. You and your friend should be particularly careful. Don't go out,' he emphasized, and hung up.

Wali returned to his place wondering why he and Akbar were specifically advised to remain indoors. 'Were they any different?' he wondered. Somehow, they spent the day and were relieved when it became dark. They shared the food the foreman had brought for himself and then scattered to go to sleep. The shops and restaurants outside had begun to open, but throngs of people could be still seen, standing in groups.

The charming boy chose to sleep in the office. Akbar slept in the back seat of a car and Wali prepared a bed on the cot. The fourth boy went out despite Wali's forbiddance.

Wali was suddenly awoken by the sounds of a violent struggle. He sat up in his bed, looking around in confusion. He realized that the noise was coming from the office. He had been leery of Akbar's designs during the past few days and jumped to his feet, hoping that his worst fears hadn't come true. He ran towards the office. As he reached it, the door burst open and the young boy emerged in a bloody mess. His shirt was torn and he was bleeding from a gash across his cheek. Coughing and screaming for help, he ran towards the gate. Wali stood in shock, watching him go out. Then Wali turned his face and saw Akbar emerging from the office, blood on his sleeves and a knife in his hand.

'What have you done?' Wali could barely speak, but he kept repeating the question.

Akbar, trembling like a dry leaf in the wind, managed to plead, 'Let us run away, Wali. Let us go back to our village.'

Wali could hardly hear him.

'Let us run away, Wali. Come with me, please,' he cajoled.

Wali quickly turned and ran towards his cot. It took him a few moments to put on his shoes. Then he started groping for his gun, which had fallen down on the floor while he was asleep. He looked for it in a frenzy and finally found it. At that moment, the gate crashed open and a mob entered. The young boy pointed towards Akbar, who ran towards Wali but was intercepted by the crowd. They threw him on the floor and began mauling him. Wali saw a man snatching his knife and repeatedly stabbing him in a fit of hate the likes of which Wali had never seen before. Then, they doused moribund Akbar with kerosene oil and set him on fire. Some of them turned towards Wali, who had his gun ready. He fired repeatedly, in quick succession. One of the attackers fell to the ground while the others ran for cover. Wali heard sirens screaming to a halt outside and saw policemen rushing in. The attackers quickly jumped over the boundary wall and he was left standing, gun in hand and two dead bodies a few yards away. One was his childhood friend, body still smoldering and emitting the stench of burning meat. Wali turned his head and vomited on his bed. As the police locked handcuffs around his wrists, he was still retching.

Nineteen

Comrade Haider arrived early at the venue. He was happy to see the arrangements Rizvi's men had made but his heart was heavy. Afzal had called him the night before, while he was revising his speech, and told him about Akbar's lynching and Wali's arrest. He now went around the tents that had been erected and looked at the rags laid down for people to sit on. The stage had been given special attention. Red carpets, ornate chairs and a public address system. He took a chair on the stage and started waiting, looking at hawkers arriving to set up their shops. An hour later, he saw the first contingent arriving in two trucks and he smiled with satisfaction. Soon, others also arrived. People from Mallah and Mohano, Sama and Jatt communities led by their leaders whom Comrade Haider knew well. He welcomed them warmly and ushered them to their seats. Beating drums and dancing to the beat, the villagers arrived at the venue. They sat down on dusty rugs, upbeat about their efforts to save their lands from a canal of toxic water.

A while later, Jannu also arrived with his community representatives. Comrade Haider waved to him from the stage and got a warm response. His presence was a source of satisfaction for

Jannu and his compatriots. He was their savvy leader who could outsmart anyone. Jannu gathered his compatriots—Shani, Dino, Moti, Mehar and Jugnu—and they all sat down in the front row closest to the stage. There were many people on the stage, people in suits and ties communicating in a foreign language. Amongst them were bankers and representatives of the construction company, including Rizvi and a few government officials in their trademark national dress and black waistcoats. A few local politicians were also seated on the stage. Jannu was surprised to see the camaraderie among the disparate groups on the stage. They shook hands and laughed as if they had known each other for a long time. Jannu was unable to read the occasional glances the people on the stage threw upon the people sitting below on dusty rugs and chanting themselves hoarse with slogans. The chanting was so loud and persistent that it appeared impossible to silence them until multiple appeals from the stage finally had their effect and the people calmed down to listen to the speakers.

First to speak was a politician who thrived on vague agendas. His speech was fuzzy and overly emotional. He threatened to start a bloody revolution if the government remained oblivious to the problems of the wetlands. His speech was so nearly irrelevant that people hardly clapped when he finished. Then came the government official, who managed to exceed the first speaker in vagueness and incertitude. He was booed off the stage by the irate crowd. The next speaker was the bank representative. He spoke calmly, free of emotional tirades, and won the attention of the people. He dwelled precisely upon the apprehensions of the people about the flaws of the link canal and announced that the bank would refuse to release funds if the flaws were not removed.

'It is you who matter and we promise to work with you,'

he declared and received thunderous applause from the gullible assembly of villagers.

Others came and spoke and finally the representative of the people, Comrade Haider, was invited to enlighten the participants. The crowd hushed to listen to one of their own. He spoke with dignity and explained the good and bad of the canal. Dwelling on the thousands of hectares of waterlogged up-country, he outlined the benefits of the canal and then spoke of its ecological effects on the wetlands due to the admixture of industrial effluents and pesticides in its water. Finally, he spoke of his and the participants' resolve to stand steadfast until the issue was resolved. Then, in a surprise move, he asked the crowd to raise their hands if they accepted him as their sole arbiter to resolve the issue. The crowd raised their hands in unison and stood up for an ovation, their applause seemingly interminable. He congratulated himself on a successful political legerdemain and returned to his seat. He was welcomed by a smiling Rizvi who warmly shook his hand.

'Now we can talk,' Rizvi whispered in his ear.

The master of ceremonies announced that as further negotiations were to be held, Jannu and his compatriots should come to the adjoining tent to meet Comrade Haider. This meeting lasted for another couple of hours. The villagers were adamant that the whole project had to be abandoned. Haider stressed the impossibility of this and reminded them of the millions the government had already invested under the pressure of the farmers of waterlogged lands upcountry. He pleaded with them to soften their demands and agree upon something that was achievable. On their insistence, Comrade Haider had to give in.

'Okay, okay. We will talk to them. Important government officials are here and they have been given a mandate to find a solution. I will take one of you with me so that you will not feel deceived. We will try to achieve the best we can. Now, who will come with me?' he asked.

After a brief discussion, they nominated Jannu and left saying they would wait outside while the two of them negotiated with the government officials. Once left alone with Jannu, Haider transformed his mien to that of a worried man. He sat closer to Jannu and put his arm around his shoulders.

'Before I left the city, I received some very worrying news about Wali,' he said in a sombre tone.

Jannu was taken aback. 'Wali? My son?' he asked impatiently.

'Yes, Wali. Your son,' he replied.

'Is he alright?' Jannu asked eagerly.

'He is in police custody,' Haider revealed.

Jannu was at a loss for words for a few moments. 'Police custody? Why?' he finally asked.

'For murder,' Haider said, and Jannu stared at him in disbelief. 'He came to me a few days ago. He had another boy, Akbar, with him. He asked me to find a job for him. Thinking that he had come with your permission, I found them jobs at a motor garage. The garage was attacked last night by a mob. His friend was burned alive and Wali killed a person in self-defence. The police found him standing a few feet away from the dead body with a gun in his hand.'

Jannu's eyes welled up with tears and he started sobbing bitterly like a child. Haider consoled him in a futile effort.

'Oh my… Oh my… I am doomed. I am doomed,' Jannu kept saying as he sobbed. He was devastated.

'We will fight his case in the court and he will be a free man. I am with you, Jannu. Now please calm down and help me get this issue of the canal out of the way,' Haider said.

It took Jannu quite a while to stop his tears. 'I am a poor man, Haider. I don't have the resources to hire lawyers and enter legal battles. I can hardly earn a living,' he said in grief.

'I will take care of everything. Just do as I tell you.'

Haider held Jannu's hand and nudged him out. Jannu obeyed like a child. It was dusk and the farmers were getting restless to leave. Their faces covered in dust and their clothes crumpled, they had waited a whole day to know the outcome of their efforts. Finally, Haider emerged, hand in hand with Jannu, and announced that the government was not prepared to abandon the project but had agreed to build a weir on the link canal. This weir would effectively prevent backflow from the sea even during high tide. He told them it was now for them to accept or reject the solution. He advised them to accept it, but if they chose not to, he stood with them and was ready to join them in a long struggle during which they could lose their livelihoods and face long terms in jail. Undecided and disillusioned, the people embarked on the return journey to their villages. They rushed to hitch rides on donkey and camel carts. The luckier ones were picked up by trucks and lorries. Others took to walking back, in long rows on both sides of the road, still discussing their gains and losses.

Comrade Haider offered a lift back home to a sullen Jannu. He drove in silence for a few miles, overtaking the long lines of villagers trudging back home on both sides of the narrow road. Jannu was lost in his thoughts, vacantly staring at the villagers who waved at them as they drove past. They waved back, Jannu half-heartedly and Haider excitedly with a broad smile. Before leaving, Haider had one final meeting with Rizvi, which had proved to be more rewarding than his expectations.

'Did we deceive them?' Jannu thoughtfully murmured,

and Haider's mind drifted away from the fruit of his political legerdemain.

'They would not wave to you if you had,' Haider replied, and then added, 'moreover, you should better think of your own problem now.'

'Yes. You are right,' Jannu replied with a sigh. 'It will be hard to break the news to his mother.'

'Don't worry. I am with you all the way,' Haider said.

His being with Jannu was not of much use when Nooran and Marvi heard the news. Nooran threw herself to the ground and rolled in the dust, crying loudly. Then she threw fistfuls of mud into her hair, cursing Jannu for this misfortune. She tore away his shirt and repeatedly slapped him on his chest. Haider could only stand and watch, not knowing what to do. Marvi, though equally grieved, remained dignified in mourning the loss. Next day, Nooran and Jannu accompanied Comrade Haider to the city. Marvi was sent to stay with a relative.

They met Wali in a police lockup. He had lost all his bravado and looked like a scared sparrow in a cage. Nooran hugged him and wept for a long time, holding him tight against her chest. After the meeting, Haider took them to a lawyer. His office was located on the second floor of a dilapidated building in a busy bazaar. The stairs were narrow and dimly lit. The air in the lawyer's office was stale and heavy with smoke. The process of hiring him was tedious and his fee was exorbitant. The fee was paid by Haider, but from Jannu's share of the money. Two days later, the lawyer called and told Haider that a date had been fixed for the first hearing, which was to be after two months. Thus started Jannu's arduous journey towards Wali's release from jail. They met Wali once more in the lockup, where they were told that he was to be shifted to jail on police remand and further meetings would not be possible. Nooran and Jannu returned to the village the next day.

The following month, Comrade Haider flew off to London, a safe haven for the politicians of his ilk and their ill-gotten wealth. He planned to request asylum on the basis of an imaginary threat to his life and was sure it would be granted. Jannu went twice to his home, but a servant, the sole inhabitant of the house then, told him that the Comrade was unlikely to return anytime soon. Jannu was left alone to pursue Wali's trial. He came and went. The courts kept changing. The schedule of hearings and the lawyer was difficult to find in the overcrowded premises of the courts, which were full of con men, extortionists and witnesses for hire. Jannu, a stranger to the legal charade, kept spending money, bribing policemen to let him talk to his son in custody and the court clerk for early dates for hearings and for his travel and lodging. He lost a huge amount of money when, after his lawyer developed metastatic cancer of the prostate and fell ill, Jannu had to hire a new lawyer who asked for an equally exorbitant fee. One day, he was told that Wali's case had been transferred to a court in another city and Wali to another jail. His second lawyer flatly refused to travel three hundred miles every month to follow the case. He also refused to return the money he had taken and invited Jannu to challenge him in court for this. He had to hire yet another lawyer and travel to yet another city to claim justice. His money rapidly depleted. Heartbroken, the family accepted the predicament as fait accompli and took to permanent mourning.

The work on the outflow drain continued unabated. The canal had arrived closer to the lake. People stopped thinking about it and concentrated on their livelihoods instead. They came to terms with their insignificance. Bachal continued to visit Jannu's place regularly, bringing him grains and sugar and making inroads into their hearts as a sincere friend and sympathizer. Nooran had pleaded with Jannu many times to seek his help in locating and releasing their son, but Jannu demurred because he was reluctant to ask for his favour in exchange for their hospitality, which they could offer because of all the money and food Bachal gave them.

Marvi had begun to feel comfortable in his presence because of her growing familiarity with the selfless and innocuous old man. The flautist still came to the lake during the night every once in a while to play the flute, rekindling her love and resolve for union with him. To her good fortune, the subject of her marriage had not arisen. Even if it did, she was determined to refuse. She hoped, waited and continued loving Murad, cocooned within herself, away from the bitterness of life and sad thoughts of a brother in jail.

Wali had also resigned himself to a life in jail. Surprisingly, no one who knew the man he had killed came to fight his case. His pleas of self-defence, however, didn't make any difference and he was condemned to permanent imprisonment. His father had come to see him every once in a while, but he was so frequently shifted from one jail to another that he presumed his family had now lost track of him. He was finally brought to a different jail on a seemingly permanent basis but did not know how to inform his family. He could not make a phone call because there were no phones in those villages and could not write a letter because bush houses do not have addresses. Captivity had mellowed him, and because of his good behaviour he was posted, ironically, to the prison garage, where police vehicles were brought for repair. There he met his mentor, an experienced mechanic who soon developed a liking for Wali because of his good manners.

'In this world, you need money to live like a human being. The safest way to earn money is to work hard,' his would-be mentor told him.

Wali started doing just that and put his heart and mind into his work.

Twenty

With his face covered to avoid the blazing sun, Jannu was lounging in his gently-rocking boat, reminiscing over the events of the past three years. He remembered the day when he was asked to plant mangrove saplings by someone from the city who had introduced him to the issue of the canal. He recalled with fondness the initial stages of their evolving movement against it. That brought forward the memory of Comrade Haider and he smiled bitterly. He had not heard from him again. The canal had started functioning and was brimming with black-coloured flowing water, which emitted a strange acrid odour that spread to a wide area with diminishing intensity. The plants and grass in its vicinity were withering, slowly but inexorably. Many herdsmen had migrated from the area because of diminishing fodder for the animals and the farmers sulked because their crops were stunted and the yield was low.

There was another reason for bad crops. It had not rained for the past two years. The clouds rushed past the skies of the wetlands like travellers hurrying through haunted ruins. This year, the summer had been exceptionally hot. The air remained still and mirages danced over the heath. So did the trees. Not a leaf moved.

Thirsty sparrows flew around in search of water with their beaks open. Stray dogs dozed in whatever shade they found. Streets in the villages and hamlets across the delta remained deserted with children rarely coming out to play. People prayed for rain as they sweltered in the heat. Only a generous rainfall could bring relief. This was in the making.

Somewhere on the surface of the Arabian ocean, convection currents had developed and grown stronger over the ensuing days. Warm air started rising, carrying water vapour with it. Cooler air rushed to fill the void, and, as it did so, it spiraled with the earth's rotation, creating a vortex. The vortex churned and rose, gaining speed by the moment. It was being watched by satellites and radar stations as it widened to several kilometres in diametre. A storm was born, and as it intensified, the weathermen watching it elevated it in status to a cyclone and gave it a name. The eye of the cyclone was identified and its course calculated. Urgent warnings were issued and concerned authorities asked to urgently start evacuating the littoral area. Ominous clouds gathered in the sky over Jannu's wetlands and strong winds started blowing across it. Flashes of lightning zigzagged across the darkening sky, leaping down to earth, thundering as they did so. It began to rain.

The whole area came to life. People laughed and shouted in excitement, congratulating each other. Children came out into the open to drench themselves in the rain. The grown-ups too let the torrents thrash the heat out of their bodies. The scorched earth soaked the water with the same eagerness as the human beings. Trees and shrubs appeared greener as the dust washed off their leaves. Farmers looked up at the clouds and exclaimed repeatedly how the rain would be good for the crops. They could now hope for greener pastures.

Sitting in his boat, Jannu watched the bubbles forming, drifting and then vanishing and analogized it to the story of life. He stayed in his boat and enjoyed the rainfall. When it grew stronger, he decided to leave, hurriedly tying the rope to a peg. He ran towards his house, praying that the harsh weather would spare it. Far away in the ocean, the cyclone started to drift towards land. The weathermen's warnings took on a hysterical tone as the possibility of landfall became imminent.

When Jannu reached home, water had already pooled in the courtyard. Nooran was heaping their possessions on a cot in the room, the ceiling of which was already dripping. He had secured a tarpaulin on his roof for a day like this, but it appeared to have been displaced by the wind. He placed a ladder against the wall to secure it again with rope. The torrents of rain made it hard for him to keep his eyes open and the tarpaulin, though wet and heavy, billowed up repeatedly with the wind. Nevertheless, he was able to tie the rope to the projecting logs. Once done with that, he descended the stairs, failing to notice that the waterproof tarpaulin had slackened and water was beginning to accumulate in it.

'Can you make a cup of tea for me?' he asked Nooran, placing the ladder near the door.

'Find me dry twigs to light a fire and I will make the tea,' Nooran shouted back over the noise of a violent storm.

Jannu realized that everything was wet. All the household's items were either floating on water or drenching in rain. 'Where is Marvi?' he asked, dashing the idea of a hot cup of sweet tea.

'The goats have run away. She has gone to get them back,' Nooran replied. 'Come and help me lift this box. The water is rising.'

The wind had transformed into a gale and torrential rain had raised a curtain of water in front of his eyes. The water had been flowing into the room and was now ankle-deep. Thundering clouds gathered and lightning leapt down, a single stem dividing into branches as it did so.

'I don't like it, Jannu,' Nooran said in apprehension.

'It will stop soon. It always does,' Jannu replied.

'I have never seen clouds and rain like this in all my life,' Nooran said, looking at the sky.

Before Jannu could respond, Marvi entered.

'I couldn't find the goats,' she told her father.

'Did you look for them well?' Nooran asked Marvi.

'I wasn't playing all this time,' Marvi retorted.

'I will go look for them when the rain slows down. They wouldn't have gone far,' Jannu interrupted.

'I saw many people going in that direction,' Marvi reported, pointing in the direction opposite the sea.

'You did?' Jannu asked in surprise.

'Yes. They were carrying their things with them,' she said.

'Just men?' Jannu asked again.

'Everyone. Women and children too,' Marvi answered.

He saw Nooran looking at him with enquiring eyes. 'Are they expecting a flood?' she asked in a worried voice.

'Maybe,' Jannu replied.

'Why don't you go and find out?' She was irked by his reply.

'The closest village is one kilometre away. You want me to go out in this weather?' He was equally irked by her suggestion, still optimistic that the rain would stop soon.

'Did you put the grain into plastic bags?' he asked Nooran.

'I have placed the sacks on a cot. I hope the water will not rise that high. If it does, there is no use putting them in plastic bags anyway,' she answered.

'I think we should do that. Come Marvi,' he said, and hurried towards the room.

They were in the habit of stuffing empty plastic bags into the crevices in the brush walls. Marvi extracted a folded bundle and came to the cot where Nooran had placed the grain sacks. One by one, the two of them filled the plastic bags with grain, sugar and flour and hung them on the projecting pieces of wood in the walls. Outside, Nooran looked at the clouds in apprehension as the rain kept lashing and thunder kept roaring across the sky. Marvi noticed that the ceiling had begun sagging under the weight of the water on the tarpaulin. She pointed it out to Jannu, who threw a cursory look towards it.

'It should hold,' he said, with a wave of his hand.

Then, he heard someone shouting his name. All three of them rushed to the door. They found Jannu's cousin, Moti, standing there trying to protect himself from the rain with a plastic sheath over his head.

'What brings you here in this weather?' Jannu shouted.

'Leave the house. Everyone is going,' Moti shouted back. 'Everyone says there is going to be a flood.'

'Where are they going?' Jannu asked.

'Any place where water will not reach them. Come on. Hurry up. My family is also leaving. I rushed here to take you with me,' Moti emphasized.

'Wait. We will come with you,' Nooran said, and rushed to grab her belongings, but Jannu held her wrist, indicating her to wait.

'Who said there is going to be a flood?' Jannu asked Moti.

In reply, Moti helplessly spread his arms and looked up to the sky. 'Can't you see it coming?'

'You go. We will follow you,' Jannu said dismissively.

'Don't complain later that no one warned you,' Moti replied as he rushed back.

A few yards away, he had already disappeared into the rain.

'Let us go with them, Jannu. Hurry or we will lose them,' Nooran pleaded hysterically.

'Go where?' Jannu screamed. 'Many of them will drown or get bitten by snakes before they reach highland. There will be no food, no water for those who survive.'

'Where will we go if the water rises?' Nooran screamed back in anger.

Jannu hesitated for a few moments, not knowing what to say. Then his face lit up with optimism. 'The tree. We can safely spend a few days in our tree. We can sit and recline in its branches. We would be close to our home and our boat. We will climb the tree if the water rises.'

This consoled Nooran a little. 'But I can't climb the tree,' she said sheepishly.

'Come. I will help you climb it. You can sit down and rest,' he said, grabbing the bamboo ladder.

They came to the tree and Jannu placed the ladder against its trunk. He helped Nooran climb and then followed her to choose a perch for her. Nooran was happier on the tree. The leaves impeded the harshness of the rain and at least she could sit. A yard away from her was a blanket that had been firmly secured in place, stretching between bifurcating trunks in what had functioned as a hammock for her son. Wali had been fond of spending hot afternoons sleeping in the hammock. Jannu descended after having dealt with Nooran.

'Let's fill the plastic bottles with water and bring our food. We can store these things in the tree so we do not need to come down to the house all the time,' he said to Marvi, and both of them went back to the house.

Marvi started pouring water from the pitchers into the plastic bottles and Jannu went into the room. He failed to notice the sagging ceiling or hear the roof creak under the weight of the water slowly filling the tarpaulin.

Twenty-one

Just a few miles away the cyclone made its landfall and the storm intensified. Stronger winds and giant waves began battering the shore. The high surf destroyed the weir on the canal and entered it in a violent backlash, which burst through the banks of the canal and flooded the land. Oceanic brine mixed with the toxic water of the canal in this onslaught. The houses that had survived the gale were washed away. People started fleeing in panic. Many lost their lives to falling trees, others were crushed when their homes collapsed or drowned in the rising water.

Jannu was lucky to escape a similar fate when his roof came down. Marvi heard the crash and her father screaming in agony moments later. She darted towards the room and saw her father under a heap of logs, crying in pain. She was quick in her response. She hurriedly removed the smaller logs first and found Jannu's arm trapped under the heaviest log. She held the end of the log with both her hands and heaved it away from Jannu's body. Then, she helped him crawl out of the room and noticed that his right forearm was deformed below the elbow. Fortunately, she was familiar with what the villagers did for broken bones. She found a slab of wood and tore off a long strip from her shawl. She placed Jannu's arm on the slab and wrapped it tight with the strips of cloth, knotting it at the end. With Jannu's left arm over her shoulders, she supported his weight and brought him out of the house. They came to the tree and Jannu managed to climb into Wali's hammock. Nooran was alarmed to see his broken arm and started crying at their helplessness.

Marvi quickly returned to the house. She retrieved the bottles of water and then, stepping over the fallen logs, entered what had been their room just a few moments ago. She frantically looked for the plastic bags of grains and sugar, but most were trapped under the logs. She could rescue only a small sack of jaggery. With this and the bottles of water she returned to the tree, hoping that someone would come to help. The water was rising rapidly and deep in her heart she knew that no one would be available for days to come.

The onslaught of wind and waves continued for a few hours until the eye of the cyclone closed on itself. The torrential rain continued. The water of the canal kept flooding the lands. Hordes of people fleeing from the rising water trudged towards embankments and levees with their possessions. Goading their animals and nudging their children, they waded through water in a seemingly endless journey. The men carried their old on their backs and the women supported buckets on their heads, the contents of which varied from live chicken and grains to small babies. Smaller children came sitting in large cauldrons or clinging to empty pitchers as floaters. Some had secured inflated tubes of tractor wheels to upturned cots and brought their families sitting on these. Improvisation and hope were their only assets in the calamity they faced. There was only water as far as their anxious eyes could see. A dark day gave way to a darker night, but the people kept walking because there was nowhere to sit.

~

Marvi lived through a difficult night in the tree. Insects persistently bothered her and kept her awake. She kept telling her mother not to go to sleep and responded to her father who huddled in the hammock, groaning with pain. She could hardly see in the darkness as she sat and waited for dawn to arrive. She was desperately missing her brother in the family's dire state. She was just a girl of a tender age, left alone to tend to her sick father and a hysterical mother and not a square metre of dry land to put her foot on.

'I must find help or we will die,' she thought to herself.

After what seemed like an eternity, dawn arrived. When it was bright enough to see, she discovered, to her horror, that they were not alone in their tree. Hundreds of spiders were keeping them company. That explained what had been persistently annoying her during the night. Forced out of their burrows by water, the spiders had hopped onto the tree for refuge. There was nothing she could do. She went closer to her parents and gave them pieces of jaggery to eat and water to drink. Then she descended from the tree, feeling for the ground with her foot immersed in water. The water came up to her waist. She looked towards the house and found all that was left of it were a few logs and planks, floating in the water. She waded towards the lake to find someone to help, but found nothing except water, in every direction. She waded towards the submerged thicket and found the carcass of one of her goats. The rain had slowed down and the clouds in the sky were now thinner. The wind had also died down, leaving behind a gentle breeze carrying a strange acrid smell. Despondent and fearful, she waded back to the tree.

'Did you find anyone?' Nooran asked her in a weak voice.

'Only our dead goat, mother,' she replied, running her fingers through her father's hair.

'What will happen to us?' her mother was on the verge of breaking down.

'We will be okay. The rain will stop soon and people will return,' she said, trying to console her.

As she fixed her eyes upon their immediate surroundings, she noticed that the spiders had begun spinning webs that stretched between the branches all around them. She broke a branch and began undoing the webs closest to her parents.

Twenty-two

The rain had slowed down but the water kept rising because of the shattered banks of the canal. The high tide had also not receded yet. By dawn, the first batch of people had arrived on the embankment called Band Wadera Nisar. It was a long embankment, a few feet in height, made by Wadera Nisar as a preventative barrier against an overflowing canal. It had failed in its purpose, there being water on both sides of a long strip of dry land, but that day it was like heaven for the people. They hurried to make encampments for their families. The women went searching for wood to light fires, some unknotted their wraps and took out kettles and whatever edibles they had managed to bring. Drinking water was passed around, the wiser ones advising to ration as no more would be available for the coming few days. Men hoisted sticks on the ground and spread plastic and linen sheets over them to protect their families from rain. Women and children squeezed into these makeshift shelters. Tea was made and generously offered in the euphoria of having survived the deluge. Two old men who had survived previous floods dimmed their spirits a bit when they went around warning people against snakes and scorpions.

'The way we came looking for dry land, holding on to our dear lives, snakes and scorpions will also come, holding on to their dear lives,' they said as they went from one group of people to the next.

By noon, a large number of people from Deh Kamharan had also arrived. They, too, busied themselves making temporary abodes and lighting fires for tea. They intermingled with the first group and shared their experiences. Some mourned the deaths of their animals and some the destruction of their homes. After some rest, a group of people volunteered to walk the few miles to the other end of the levy to find dry passage inland or shallow waters that could be crossed.

'How would you know? One can't gauge the depth of water by looking at its surface,' a villager said.

'We better wait here for help to arrive,' another suggested.

'No one will come for help in this daunting expanse of water. We should rather help ourselves,' one of the volunteers waved in dismissal and the group left in search of a way for them to proceed towards a village inland to find food and water.

More people arrived as the time passed. More fires were lit and makeshift shelters were made. The initially upbeat atmosphere did not prevail for long. A sombre mood replaced it when the people talked about loss of crops and destruction of homes. Many of them were looking for kith and kin who had failed to arrive. Some found them, some did not. Those who found them laughed in happiness, kissed and hugged each other and then sat down to describe their arduous march to safety. Those who did not were comforted by friends who suggested they must have gone somewhere else. This was an unrealistic possibility. There were no other levees or points of higher ground in the surrounding area. Their hearts were restless and they repeatedly scanned the waters for approaching figures.

Around noon a helicopter appeared in the sky with the telltale sound of its rotors drawing closer. People rushed to wave and shout to attract the attention of the people riding in it. The helicopter flew past the embankment and disappeared into the horizon. The hollering crowd watched it disappear.

'They will come back. Now that they have seen our misery, they will return with food and water.'

Some of them were optimistic, while many remained doubtful. The proposition of going further inland was gaining more and more approval as it was discussed among different groups.

'There is nothing here. No food and no water. Whatever we have brought with us will suffice for a single day. We must make it to a place where we can get some help. Soon people will start falling ill. Mosquitos in the night and snakes during the day will make it necessary to find medical help. If we don't, many will die.'

The proponents appealed vehemently and many of the listeners nodded in agreement. Then the volunteer group returned. People surrounded them, eagerly waiting for the news they had brought.

'There is no dry land and water beyond the levee is chest deep. There is nowhere else to go,' one of the volunteers announced.

Deeply disappointed, they returned to their families. The once desolate embankment looked more like a village by the time night fell. Fires were burning along its length and lanterns spread their soft light in the makeshift shelters as groups of people sat on bare ground, discussing the flood.

Twenty-three

Marvi did nothing during the day except tend to her torpid father and quietly sobbing mother. The two bottles of water she had brought were almost empty and little remained in the sack of jaggery. Jannu's condition was worsening and she noticed discolouration of his right hand. The spiders were spinning webs with great speed and she felt like a trapped insect. She had tried shouting for help, but was rewarded with silence, not even an echo. Around midday, she decided to go down and search for help again. Step by step, she moved to the trunk and placed her foot on the ladder. She was about to submerge her leg when she saw a snake lashing in the water just a yard away. She screamed and quickly withdrew her leg but could not take her eyes off the snake. She hurriedly returned to her perch, her eyes still fixed on it. As a precaution, she broke a long, thick branch and held it in her hand to prevent the snake from climbing the tree. She agonized over the possibility for a long time, stick in a tight grip and eyes on the snake. She relaxed only when she saw it climb onto a floating plank of wood. It was only a temporary reprieve as the danger was still present and close by, but she diverted her attention towards the spiders and their webs, her parents and their intensifying misery. The inside of the tree had turned grey due to the webs. The rain had reduced to a drizzle by noon and stopped entirely by dusk. She waited in her purgatory, hoping someone would come looking for them.

~

Someone was indeed looking for her, but was doing so on the levee. He had walked up and down the levee the entire day and hadn't given up when darkness shrouded the land.

'Did you find her, Murad?' his sister asked him when she saw her despondent brother return from his latest search.

'I don't think they are here,' Murad replied.

'Take some rest now. We will look for them together tomorrow,' Athee told him. She took out a piece of bread and gave it to him with some water.

'Any more left?' Murad asked.

'Only enough for another day,' Athee said.

He was about to bite into the bread, but stopped short. Extending his hand towards his sister, he offered it to her instead.

'You take it, Athee. I don't feel hungry.'

Athee smiled and looked lovingly at him. 'You have a heart of gold, my dear brother. I have eaten my share, and I insist that you should eat yours,' she said.

'I wish you could do something for my heart,' he smiled back.

'I will, Murad. She will be of age in a few months. I will go to her parents after the water recedes and we return to our homes,' she replied seriously. 'You kept your promise of not embarrassing the family, it is time for me to keep mine.'

~

Bachal had spent sleepless nights since he heard about the flood on his television. One of the channels had shown aerial footage of the havoc wreaked. For miles and miles, water had submerged houses and trees. From high above the numerous people looked like ants escaping the floods in long lines. The news coverage told of a significant death toll that was expected to rise in the coming days. The commentators spoke of the sluggish response by the concerned authorities despite pleas from meteorologists against the delay in evacuation of the littoral area. Bachal could only think of Marvi when he saw the coverage. He followed the news throughout the night but as the newscasters started to repeat the few facts and footage they had, his patience started to wane. He wondered about the fate of the girl for whom he had patiently waited for so long. The region had become inaccessible to him overnight, leaving him helpless despite his might and resourcefulness. This frustrated and angered him. He vented his anger on Mithal early the next morning.

'Do you have any idea what she means to me?' he asked Mithal.

'More than anything I know of,' Mithal replied, keeping his voice low.

'Have you bothered to find out what happened to her in the floods?' Bachal asked, grinding his teeth. 'It has been two days.'

'It was impossible, master. There is water everywhere,' Mithal tried to explain, hoping that Bachal would see reason.

'Water or fire, I want to know about her safety,' Bachal roared.

'I will try my best, master.' Mithal said and, considering it safer to leave, edged towards the door.

'Listen,' Bachal shouted and Mithal stopped in his tracks. 'Go to the area. Walk, ride the tractor or get a boat, whatever you want to do, but bring me news of her.' Bachal paused ominously. 'I will hold you responsible if she suffers any harm.'

As Mithal hurried to leave, Bachal slumped on a sofa, thinking of Marvi. He realized that she had become his obsession.

Twenty-four

The sky was an innocent shade of blue on the morning of the third day. The sun ascended across the horizon in its full glory, bathing the region in golden rays. A new day had arrived. A few of the silky spiral webs in the tree gleamed in the light that managed to filter through. More webs had loomed around Marvi and her parents. After the second sleepless night, she was on the verge of collapsing. Jannu had drifted into a coma, his hand becoming dusky blue in colour. Nooran was no better. She was in a state of stupor. Marvi knew that this could be the last day of their lives if she failed to find help. Peering through the webs, she tried to locate the snake in the water below. She saw the planks and pieces of wood floating around the ladder but didn't see the snake. She had little doubt it was still there, but she had to take the risk.

She braced to make her final effort for survival. She came down and placed her foot on the first step of the ladder that had mercifully remained in place throughout the storm. She looked for the snake once more and then descended into the water with a subdued splash. At that moment, she sensed something whip in the water a few yards away but forced herself to ignore it. She started wading towards the lake in the hope of finding her boat. She could see the top of the brushwood that grew along the lake. She covered a few hundred yards at the speed of a snail and reached the point where she expected to see the boat. She did see it, capsized and shattered. She stood for a moment in silence trying to absorb the shock. Before returning to the tree, she went towards the remains of her home in one last hope of finding the plastic sacks of food. She found one with sugar in it, but water had entered it and the sugar had turned into a syrup. She grabbed it, tightened the knot at its opening and waded back towards the tree. She suddenly stopped when she saw from a distance that the spiderwebs had fully cocooned the tree. It appeared bizarre. She was horror-struck, and it took her a while to fully accept that it was the only place for refuge. Wondering how anyone would find them in there, she started wading again. The last traces of hope deserted her. With no alternative available, she climbed the tree.

'Did you find anyone?' her mother asked her weakly.

'No one, mother. Our boat is also destroyed,' she said, and came closer to let her sip from the sack she had rescued. Then she trickled the syrup into the open mouth of her father, covered his face with her shawl and returned to her perch.

～

The embankment was becoming crowded due to the arrival of more people who came in the hope of finding food and water distributed by rescuers. Every time a new group arrived, Murad went looking for Marvi. By evening, he had come back to Athee. They sat together to finish the last piece of bread Athee had and were eating in silence when they saw a man walking towards them.

'Are you the lad who has been looking for someone from Deh Kharo?' he enquired.

'Yes, yes. I am the one,' Murad eagerly replied.

The man sat down and smiled. 'My name is Moti and I am from Deh Kharo. Who are you looking for?' he asked.

This time Athee spoke. 'We are looking for Jannu. Do you know him?'

'Yes, I do. I am his cousin. But he didn't accompany us. I went to his house before we abandoned the village, but he wouldn't come with us,' he informed them.

'Why?' Athee could not resist asking.

'He is like that; a loner. He even built his house far away from the village,' Moti explained. Then he threw a curious glance at Murad and touched his flute. 'Are you the boy who used to come to the lake to play his flute?'

Athee hurried to reply. With a broad smile she shook her head. 'No, it must be someone else. He is only learning,' she lied.

'Okay, then. I hope you have your answer.' He got up, waved and walked away.

Both of them sat silently for a while, agonizing over Jannu's foolishness. Murad was still shaking his head in disbelief when he saw a boat approaching the levee. Suddenly, he got up and darted towards the point where it was expected to touch land. Athee called out to him but he ignored her and kept running at full speed. The boat reached the levee and two women and a child stepped out. A man stepped into the water and pushed the boat on to land. It was a flat-bottomed punt. The man placed the punting pole alongside the boat and, picking up his luggage, joined the women to encamp. Murad stood watching them. He saw them mingling with people and saw the man going away, perhaps to find his friends and relatives. Once he was out of sight, Murad hastened towards the boat. After a moment of hesitation, he took off his shoes and threw them into it and pushed it back into the water. Then he picked up the punting pole and with powerful thrusts against the earth under the water, he drifted away from the levee. By the time Athee arrived, panting and anxious, he was too far to reach.

Twenty-five

Once beyond the reach of the boat's owner, Murad realized his difficulties. He was awkwardly propelling the punt, unable to do it as smoothly as the owner had done. Initially, he stood in the middle of the boat, but moved to the back when he recalled the position of the owner. Still, he kept moving, repeatedly immersing the pole and heaving into a forward thrust. He had problems in maintaining his balance too. But he persisted with dour determination. To err is to learn, and he was learning quickly. Now a few hundred yards away from the levee, he looked back and saw a small crowd gathered on the shore, watching him go. He looked ahead towards the misty, featureless expanse of water. The flood had wiped away the landmarks and water had submerged whatever could withstand its onslaught. The light of the stars was dim, forcing him to strain his eyes to be able to see through the haze. Every once in a while, he looked back towards the levee to fight off the creeping feeling of loneliness in the dreary night, but the light of the lanterns and the outlines of embankments were fading away. He was alone. Unable to swim and a novice at propelling the punt, he had started to feel nervous at the thought of dire possibilities, but Marvi's face was a compelling lure. He had seen her only twice, but the memory was as sharp as engraving in stone. Murad had been so moonstruck by that first encounter that nothing else mattered more to him since that day. He had dared many dark nights when he came to the lake to play the flute for her, hoping that she would recognize the melody and remain tethered to him. The boat kept skimming and he kept thinking until suddenly it collided with something and stopped moving. He went forward and saw the carcass of a cow, its body bloated and upturned, its rigid legs pointed skywards. The stench was overwhelming. Retching and fighting for air, he receded as quickly as he could with his face contorted in a grimace. He redirected the boat with some difficulty and started heaving once more.

After what seemed like an eternity, he noticed the outline of a tree. Propelling the punt with new-found vigour, he came closer and felt his energy drain away when he found himself confronted by an eerie sight. For a while he stood there paralyzed, staring at the tree, which appeared to be wrapped in a thin grey fabric. Then, he gathered courage and moved towards it. He took his punt around the tree, trying to understand the bizarre sight when he noticed the ladder and stopped. Could she be inside this damnation?

'Marvi?' he called in a tremulous voice.

There was no answer. Dreading the thought of her death, he shouted out her name in a long cry. He shouted till his throat choked. In his hysteria, he failed to hear the responding voices.

'Help us, please. Don't go away,' he heard a female pleading.

He stopped the boat near the ladder and climbed up in a frenzy. Then he saw her face. They stared at each other for an ecstatic moment.

'What took you so long, flautist?' Marvi whispered.

She had yearned to see his face for a long time. Here he stood as her saviour, come to rescue her from her hell.

Twenty-six

By dusk, Mithal had arrived in the small town which was the gateway to the wetlands. A narrow metalled road led from the town into the region. It branched and rebranched, reducing to dirt tracks which snaked towards hundreds of small villages and hamlets. He stopped his motorcycle near the small hospital in the hope of finding the injured and the sick amongst the flood-affected people being brought for treatment. The hospital was as deserted as ever. He saw army trucks arriving and entering the premises.

A person standing nearby remarked sarcastically, 'What do they hope to find here except heaps of rubbish and a few stray dogs?'

His companion disagreed. 'No, they will find a lot more,' he said.

The first person looked at him enquiringly.

'They will find broken beds, expired medicine, foraging cats and hash-smoking junkies too,' he explained, and both of them broke out into a laughter.

Mithal could also not resist a smile. 'Is there a hotel nearby?' he asked them, and one of them pointed towards a dilapidated two-story building.

Mithal decided to stay the night there and planned to drive into the wetlands in the morning. He paid for a room for himself and then took a walk through the bazaar hoping to find a lead that he could follow in his effort to find Marvi.

~

They arrived at the levee at dawn. Marvi had sat silently during the journey, looking at Murad without blinking and imbibing the bliss of the moment. Murad saw army rafts bringing in more displaced people. One of the dinghies had a red crescent painted over it. As he slowly approached dry land, he saw Athee waving in excitement. The man standing next to her looked familiar to him. 'Was he the owner of the boat?' Murad wondered. He was, as Murad discovered when he set foot on the levee. But to his surprise, the man smiled good-heartedly and hurried toward them. Athee hugged Marvi with the intensity of a mother hugging her lost child. Her face pressed against Athee's bosom, Marvi felt deeply protected and didn't move away till she felt Murad tap on her shoulder.

'My turn,' he said, and Athee hugged Murad with the same intensity.

'My brave boy. My brave boy,' she said, while he clung to her like a child.

The boat owner, who had helped Nooran come up, said to Athee, 'The old man looks dead.'

'He is alive but very sick. We have to take him to the hospital,' Murad replied. 'Can you lend me your boat one more time?'

'It's yours, my boy, but I had better come with you in case you need help,' the man replied.

'That would be very nice of you. It was difficult to handle,' Murad said.

'I will come with you,' Marvi said to Murad, and enquiringly looked to Athee.

'Go ahead, my child. I will look after your mother,' Athee said.

Soon the three of them were on their way, the man propelling the punt deftly and at greater speed. Jannu was in a coma, oblivious of his surroundings.

'Where are we heading?' Murad asked the boat owner.

'We are going towards the town. I hope we can find some help while we are on our way,' the boat owner replied. 'The water will be shallow further ahead and this boat would be of no use.'

Marvi sat close to her father, nudging him to open his eyes. She was in tears because of his dismal condition. Murad came to her and held her hand.

'He is going to be alright,' he said. 'I promise you. Please don't cry.'

Still in tears, she looked at him and smiled. With her pink lips stretching over her pearl white teeth and dimples appearing in her cheeks, she looked even prettier. This barely mitigated his worry. He knew they were in a race against time. The boat owner was equally anxious, pushing his pole against the bottom as forcefully as he could. Then Murad saw an army dinghy and started waving and shouting frantically. He was seen by the two men in the raft and they changed direction, moved in a wide arc and came closer to them.

'We have a very sick man,' Murad shouted and they came closer till the side of the raft rubbed against the side of the punt.

They craned their necks and carefully stepped into the punt. With Murad's help, they transferred Jannu onto the raft. Murad and Marvi also shifted to the raft with them.

'Thank you so much. I owe a debt of kindness to you,' Murad

said to the punt owner, waving his hand in much gratitude.

The man smiled and waved back. 'I wish you two happiness in life,' he said and immersed his pole to push away.

Twenty-seven

Mithal woke up early and hurriedly prepared to leave. He knew his journey would be difficult, if not impossible. He bought a bottle of water and placed it on the carrier of his motorcycle before driving away. When he reached the hospital, he entered it with the intention of checking out any arrivals. He was amazed to see the change. It had been turned into a functioning facility overnight. There were nurses in the wards and even surgeons in the operating rooms. He saw rows of beds with clean bed sheets in the ward, but no patients had arrived. He decided against waiting at the hospital and drove on.

When Mithal reached the bazaar, he stopped and looked around for displaced families but found none. He drove two miles further and then turned left on the road towards the wetlands. After a short while he saw army trucks heading towards the town. The army had started evacuating the affected regions. He saw an army vehicle parked on the roadside. He stopped.

'How is the road further ahead?' he asked.

The man pointed towards the wheels of his vehicle and Mithal noticed large lumps of mud stuck to the tires and mudguards. 'All mud,' the man said. 'Beyond fifteen kilometres of this is water. You will need a boat.'

Mithal was utterly disappointed. He knew he had to find Marvi for his master and soon. He did not dare go back without news of her well-being. He stood there undecided for quite some time, tapping the petrol tank of his motorcycle in thought.

'Go back. You don't have a chance,' the same man recommended. 'Who are you looking for? Your mother? Parents?'

Mithal shook his head, surprised at his inability to lie. 'A girl,' he said.

'Your wife? Fiancée?' the man asked insistently.

'My master's fiancée,' Mithal said, and was sure he had not lied.

The man shook his head, smiling. 'Tell your master to wait and pray she survives this catastrophe,' the man finally said and turned away.

Mithal finally decided to go back, muttering, 'You don't know my master.'

He turned his motorcycle and sped back towards the town.

~

They arrived at the hospital sometime after sunset. The hospital was a crowded place by then. They were seen by a surgeon on arrival. He looked at Jannu's dusky purple hand and immediately declared that he would urgently need amputation for any chance of survival. Marvi looked at Murad in wide-eyed desperation.

'Can't you save his hand?' Murad asked the surgeon.

'No,' he replied flatly.

Marvi and Murad stared at each other anxiously.

'You have to decide soon if you want him to live,' the surgeon told Murad softly, but emphatically.

Murad looked at Marvi again. After some hesitation, she nodded in consent. A nurse brought a consent form while Jannu's stretcher was pushed towards the operating room. The surgeon blurted orders about crossmatching blood and some investigations and hurried towards another patient. Murad and Marvi found a bench near the operating room and sat down. After many moments of silence, Murad gently put his hand on Marvi's hand. She looked towards him.

'Are you worried?' Murad asked.

'No!' Marvi whispered back. 'You are with me?'

'But you hardly know me, Marvi,' he said.

'You took my silk scarf and then flaunted it when you were playing your flute. Then you came to meet me at my home. I remember your face better than the lines on my palm.' She waved her hand in front of him with a mischievous smile.

'I have lived with that memory all these years,' he said dreamily.

'Why didn't you come to meet me again!' she complained.

'Athee told me not to be a cause of embarrassment to your parents,' he explained.

'She means so much to you?' Marvi asked him.

'She is my sister who brought me up like a mother. She does,' he told her.

'She was like a mother to me too.' Marvi remembered the long, warm hug Athee gave her.

Murad suddenly became serious. 'Promise me something, Marvi.'

'Whatever you say,' she said, turning to look at his face.

'We will live and die together,' he said.

'That is something I promised to myself a long time ago. I give you my promise.' Her voiced choked with emotion and her eyes moistened.

'Thank you, Marvi,' Murad could barely whisper back, overcome with emotions.

At that moment, Mithal entered the hospital. He parked his motorcycle and scanned the crowd of people. He went from one group to another asking about Jannu. No one seemed to know him. He went all around the premises but didn't have any luck. He returned to the gate and scanned the incoming crowds in the hope of seeing a familiar face. He stood there for a long time before deciding to go into the building. Hospitals scared him, but Bachal scared him more. He entered the ward and went from one end to the other, asking about the health of various patients from their relatives and then throwing in a query about Jannu. An hour later, hunger forced him to leave in search of food.

When Mithal exited the hospital, Jannu was brought out of the operating room. Marvi and Murad jumped to their feet and rushed forward. Jannu was still unconscious.

'We hope he will recover in a day or two,' the doctor said briefly to Murad. 'But he is still not out of danger.'

Jannu was finally shifted to a bed. Murad sat on the bench and Marvi sat towards the head of the bed, caressing Jannu's hair. They were keen to help but didn't know what to do. The ward boy brought the food trolley and started giving food to patients. Murad saw Marvi following the movements of the trolley with hopeful and hungry eyes. They brought the trolley close to Jannu but moved away. Murad called after him, asking for their share. The boy looked at him and shook his head.

'It is only for patients and your patient's bed is not on the list. He has to remain nil by mouth for a few hours,' he explained in medical jargon.

Murad could read the disappointment in Marvi's face and

realized that she had not eaten anything in the past thirty-six hours.

'I will bring you food,' he said, slipping his feet into his shoes.

'Do you have money?' Marvi asked, concerned.

'I have my flute,' he said.

'No, please don't sell your flute,' Marvi said, getting up to stop him, but he was already out of the door.

Twenty-eight

Murad reached a busy restaurant within walking distance of the hospital by dinner time. He hesitantly entered, looking around to find a potential buyer for his flute. He found men growling over their food, unlikely admirers of an instrument of warmth and beauty. He was still standing there undecided when the man behind the counter called out to him. He went up to the man, who he thought was likely the owner of the place. The man was busy taking money, counting it and placing it in a drawer. He waved at Murad to wait as he deftly fingered a short stack of bills. Finally, he turned his face towards him.

'Find a seat. There will be a few made vacant soon,' he said with professional courteousness.

'But I don't have money,' Murad responded sheepishly.

'Then?' the man asked, pointing towards a picture on the wall of a man shunning a beggar.

Murad blushed when he saw the picture. 'I have this flute to sell. It is not a cheap bamboo flute. It is made of aluminum and will fetch you good money,' he quickly explained.

The man took the flute, inspected it and then returned it. 'It is of no use to me. I can't play it and it would be hard for me to find a buyer,' he said.

Disappointed, Murad was about to leave when the man spoke again.

'But if you play it and if I like the music, I will give you food for free. You can sit in this chair.' He pointed to a chair beside the counter. 'I make you this offer because I like you.'

Murad cheerfully sat down and brought the flute to his lips. The desperate musician playing for the sake of his starving love put his soul into the song. The emanating melancholic music embodied his feelings and had instant effect on the listeners. The restaurant owner swayed along with the melody with his eyes closed. People turned their heads to see him. So did Mithal. Sitting in the far corner, he had recognized the music instantly. He listened for a few moments and then walked over to the washbasin to wash his hands.

~

Marvi was aghast at the amount of food with which Murad returned.

'How did you manage this?' she asked.

Chirping excitedly, she arranged the plastic boxes on the bench. Murad waited only long enough for Marvi to have the first bite before they both began to eat eagerly.

'It is delicious,' she said with a mouthful of bread and gravy.

'Anything is delicious when you're hungry,' Murad said. He pushed the box of rice towards her. 'Here, have some rice.'

'I would eat poison if you asked me to,' she said jokingly and opened the lid of the rice box.

Murad kept glancing at her as she ate. He didn't fail to see that although she was starving, she ate with a dignified restraint. A few yards away, there stood Mithal, grinning at this serendipity. He decided to wait until they had eaten and stepped out for a smoke.

Mithal saw Murad step out half an hour later with a plastic sack full of empty boxes, looking for a place to dump their trash. Once he was gone, Mithal walked into the ward and approached Marvi. She was astonished but happy to see him.

'How did you find us?' she asked cheerfully, rising to welcome him.

'A father will find his daughter, whatever the odds,' he said in his usual cloyingly sweet manner. He looked worriedly at Jannu and circled the bed twice. 'Don't worry. Bachal will come and take care of everything,' he said to comfort her. 'Who is the boy with you? A friend?'

'More than that,' Marvi said. She was prepared for this question, and didn't want to misrepresent her feelings.

'Relative?' Mithal asked, and was surprised when Marvi shook her head to say no. 'Then?' he asked tensely and waited for her reply.

'My saviour!' Marvi said plainly.

'And you love him?' Mithal asked unabashedly, and received an equally unabashed and confident reply.

'I worship him,' she said.

Mithal felt like he had been hit by an avalanche. He was at a loss for words as Marvi's response settled in his mind. He had been spinning webs around her for months and was seeing them brushed away in a single sweep. 'Adversity has made her outgrow her years,' he thought to himself.

Twenty-nine

A van full of uniformed policemen arrived first. Then came a truck full of personal bodyguards armed with automatic weapons. Following these two vehicles was Bachal's Land Cruiser. They all stormed out and scurried after Bachal, who was received by Mithal at the door. The crowd hurriedly split to make way for them, looking at Bachal in reverence.

Bachal entered the ward and Mithal guided him to Jannu's bed. Bachal's furious gaze was fixed on Murad's face as he approached. Murad stared back, trying to understand the disdain he felt from this stranger. He saw Marvi stand up quickly and cover her head. He, too, stood up in respect. Bachal briefly placed his hand on her head, a gesture of compassion from an elder, and then sadly looked at Mithal.

'Still unconscious?' he asked, and then angrily added, 'Why didn't you people tell me?'

'How could we? It happened so suddenly,' Marvi replied in a respectfully low voice.

'Who is this boy?' he hissed and Mithal quickly intervened.

'Master, he is the one who rescued them.'

'Hmm. That was brave of you, boy,' he said, nodding his head.

Then he pulled a few notes of currency from his pocket and offered the money to Murad, who blushed in indignation and stepped back, shaking his head in disbelief.

'Take it. This is your reward. Take it and go,' Bachal snarled.

Murad didn't move an inch. Bachal turned toward him in fury and struck him so hard that Murad staggered back. This was the cue to his bodyguards, who darted forward and started beating Murad ruthlessly. Marvi screamed and sprang at them, tearing their shirts, biting them and scratching their faces with her nails. She fought like a cougar, but they dragged Murad out of the ward anyway. Marvi wrenched herself free of Mithal's grip and bolted after them. She pounced on them once more but was repeatedly thrown back. Bleeding from her nose and the corner of her mouth, she rose again and kept fighting. Still, she failed to prevent them from throwing Murad into the truck and driving away. Mithal grabbed her by her hair and stopped her from chasing the truck on foot.

'Don't do this. They will kill him.' He shook her and shouted at her.

As Marvi stared back at him helplessly, he drove the point further loudly, emphatically.

'You don't know Bachal. They will kill him if you behave like this. Come to your senses.'

'I want him back. I want him back,' she managed to say as she sobbed bitterly.

'I will get him back for you, my daughter. This is a father's promise to his daughter,' he muttered reassuringly as he pressed her head to his chest. 'Calm down, my child. I will bring him back.'

Thirty

Conditions on the levee were rapidly deteriorating. The stench of stale water and human waste, vultures screaming in the sky, putrefying carcasses and wild dogs tearing at carrion in the vicinity made people acrimonious and edgy. They had depleted their stores of food and water and continued to sit in wait of aid. They could withstand the stench and the vultures, but it was impossible to fight hunger and thirst. They were quick to anger and fought or barked profanities at the slightest provocation. Humanity was at its lowest ebb in the face of unending adversity. Many of the sick had been evacuated, but people kept falling ill, especially the children. It was in this atmosphere that the first-aid helicopter appeared in the sky. People rose and ran towards its expected landing spot. They pushed and restrained each other, trampled the fallen women and children, barricaded adversaries and howled like animals in a mad rush for food. As the helicopter hovered lower and they saw its door open, they closed together in a mobile mass, moving where the helicopter moved, hundreds of hands stretched towards the sky. When the packets started falling, they scattered in a frenzy, vanquishing competitors with brute force. Fights broke out in which the weaker ones were eliminated from the struggle and the stronger ones gathered greater loot than they were due.

Athee watched this mayhem from a distance. She chose to keep her dignity and decided not to join the melee. Instead she sat down to watch and hope. To her good fortune, a boy running past her dropped a packet. Athee picked it up and called after him, but he didn't stop. She hurriedly tore it open. There were two small bottles of water and a packet of biscuits in it. She drank one bottle and ate two biscuits. The rest she kept for Nooran.

Meanwhile, someone had come to see Nooran. Moti had been looking for her for many days and had finally found her. Nooran was excited to be visited by one of her own and welcomed him joyously.

'So he was taken to the hospital. Who went with him? Marvi?' he asked.

'Yes, Marvi and the boy,' Nooran replied.

'Oh! I see. It must be the same boy,' he frowned.

'You know him?' Nooran was surprised.

'Everyone knows him. He was going from end to end asking about Jannu on the day we arrived,' he informed Nooran. 'You should not have allowed Marvi to go along,' he added with manifest disappointment.

'I was too sick to make decisions, but why do you say that?' Nooran was worried.

'Most of the people he asked knew neither Jannu nor him. But our people know Jannu and could guess who he was,' he said.

'How?' Nooran was getting frustrated.

'Some remembered his face from the investiture ceremony. Others figured it out when they saw the flute peeking out of his shirt's pocket. They put two and two together and concluded that it must be the same person who came to the lake at night and played his flute,' Moti said.

Nooran fell silent for a while.

'You know how people are. They gossip,' he continued.

'What about?' she asked impatiently.

'Why would a young man come looking for Jannu? It was obvious it was Marvi he was looking for,' he said emphatically.

Nooran had heard what she didn't want to hear. It was one of her own who had seeded her with anxiety and worry.

'What did they say?' Nooran could not resist asking.

'That, I don't need to tell you. You can guess very well.'

Moti's words went searing through her brain. She resented association with a person who had brought opprobrium to them through his indiscretion. She thought for a while and then said, 'I don't want to stay here with his sister. Can you take me with you?'

'Sure,' Moti said and extended his hand to help her up.

When Athee returned with her share of water and biscuits, Nooran was long gone.

Thirty-one

Marvi had dissociated herself from her surroundings and continued sulking. Mithal was Jannu's chief caretaker now. He kept cajoling Marvi but nothing assuaged her grief. She wanted Murad to come back to her at any cost. One night, when Mithal had gone home, she wrapped herself in a bed sheet and snuck out, determined to find Murad. She stepped out of the ward and found many people asleep on the premises, the occasional glow of cigarettes was the only evidence of those still awake. Slowly, she made her way towards the main gate. As she stood there deciding which direction to take, she heard Mithal's voice.

'That would be very foolish.'

She turned and saw Mithal standing a few yards behind her.

'You know what people do to women who are alone,' he said.

'I want to go to Murad,' she said, voice heavy with emotion.

Mithal was silent for a while, and then said, 'Okay. I will take you to him. I have not forgotten my promise.'

Murad sat bruised and battered on the floor of a small, empty, dimly-lit room at the police station. The policemen had dumped him there after beating him unconscious. When he came to his senses, his body hurt all over and even the slightest movement was agonizing. He lay motionless on the floor for hours until hunger forced him to crawl towards the glass of water and two plates of food someone had placed near the door. After eating the food, he had banged on the door and shouted, but no one responded. He sat down, fearful and apprehensive in the sepulchral silence that made the room feel like a grave.

He briskly raised his head from his knees when he heard footsteps approaching the room. The door opened and he saw Marvi standing in the doorway. Life returned to him and he tried to get up, but Marvi quickly reached him and made him sit back down. She touched his face tenderly and whispered his name. And just his name conveyed a thousand words to define her feelings. She placed her face against his chest and Murad wrapped his arms around her, both sitting in silence for countless moments. The warmth of their bodies conversed. They knew they were at the mercy of a virulent tide and could only hope to be thrown ashore while they were still alive and together. There were no plans or solutions they could talk about. They could only resolve. This, they did, and their bodies spoke.

Then someone knocked on the door and they quickly separated. Mithal entered, his sullen face exuding sympathy. It appeared that he had been crying. They smiled to welcome him. He sat in front of them and arranged his thoughts before he spoke.

'Now you two listen to me carefully. I hope you will believe me when I say I love this child like a father loves his daughter,' he said.

'We do, we really do,' Marvi said, holding his hand.

'You two are up against impossible odds. Bachal wants to marry this girl,' he revealed, and Marvi was so shocked she was unable to speak for a while.

'But he is an old man!' she finally protested.

'Only old men do such things, and only if they have money,' Mithal explained. 'There is no way the two of you could fight him. He could decimate both of you, and he would love to put his hands on Murad especially,' he continued. 'But... but... I am going to help you,' he announced with panache.

'How can you Mithal? You work for him.' Marvi was sceptical.

'I am his servant, not his slave,' he declared and then added, 'This will only be possible if you place absolute trust in me.'

'We do. Please believe us,' Marvi said impatiently.

Satisfied that he had their trust, he revealed his plan. 'Now this is what I want you to do. They will release Murad shortly after we go. Murad, once you are free, don't return to the hospital. Go back to wherever you came from. In due course, Marvi and Jannu will also relocate. Once this is done, I will make arrangements for the two of you to elope. You will wait for my instructions and not do anything foolish. Do you promise?' he asked.

'Yes, we promise,' both of them said eagerly in one voice.

'On a particular night I choose, Murad will come to take you. I will help you reach the port city and give you enough money to survive. From then on, you will be on your own.' He was happy to see them cheer up, and got up. 'Time to leave, Marvi.'

Marvi obediently got up and waved to Murad one final time before the two left the room. To Murad's surprise, he saw Mithal peep in again after a short while with a broad smile on his face.

'They will give you back your flute, and here is some money,' he said, flipping an envelope towards him.

Thirty-two

Murad was freed the next day. He was driven a few miles away from the town and dropped off to walk the remaining distance to Band Wadera Nawaz. He plodded a few kilometres in the mud before reaching the levee and the longing embrace of his sister. She heard his story with steely silence. Murad left out the part about their plan to elope.

After he finished, Athee simply said, 'I would have killed him if something had happened to you.'

She appeared so distant and unfamiliar when she said this that it reminded him of how she checked her gun every night before they went to sleep when he was a child. He believed her.

'Time to go home, Murad,' she said, breaking a pensive silence. 'Others are planning to return as well.'

She was right. People wanted to restart their lives. They wanted to see what had happened to their homes and grain silos and see if any of their cows and goats had survived. A small chance, they told each other, but still they hoped. Those who had not heard from their relatives were impatient to look for them. They had seen enough open sky and yearned for roofs over their heads. The unending croaking of frogs and the stench and constant fear of snakes and scorpions were now beyond their endurance. Many of them had already started packing.

~

Bachal visited Jannu a day before he was to be discharged. His amputated stump had healed well and his stitches had been removed. Jannu was finding it hard to come to terms with the loss of his working hand. Every time he wanted to do something, he extended his phantom limb, only to retract it sheepishly. He was very bitter with Marvi for letting it happen, as the nurse had told him about the signature of consent.

'You've reduced me to a beggar. I would rather be dead,' he told her repeatedly.

With his right hand gone, he missed his son more than ever. There was a lot to do in the coming days. Things he would be incapable of doing without two working hands. He needed help, paying little heed to Marvi's reassurances that she was there to help him.

'A daughter can never be a substitute for a son,' he said, giving little credit to her brave fight after he broke his arm.

He knew he had to renew his efforts to get his son out of jail and there was no better person than Bachal to help him in this. For him, it was a facile issue. He made a final decision and went to sleep, later to be woken by Mithal when Bachal arrived. Once again, he extended his phantom limb for a handshake, still only half awake. Bachal cringed at the feel of the stump, and let it go quickly.

'Are you ready to go home?' Bachal tried to sound joyous.

'I don't have a home, sir. It was washed away.'

His eyes suddenly welled up with tears as he sat up in bed. He looked so pathetic that Bachal was overwhelmed by sympathy for him. Jannu dried his eyes with his sleeve and tried to approximate his hands, a gesture of absolute obsequiousness that nevertheless looked awkward because of the absence of his hand.

'Sir, you have done us many favours. We will never be able to pay you back or thank you enough. Do me one last favours. Bring me back my son,' he beseeched Bachal.

Bachal glanced towards Marvi, who had been sitting like a statue since he arrived, her head bent and gaze fixed on the floor. He saw her briskly raise her head and look at him with supplicant eyes. Bachal looked at her until she blushed and lowered her gaze, embarrassed at the way he was looking at her.

'Do you know where he is now?' Bachal asked Mithal.

'Only that he is in a jail. Which jail, this I don't know,' Mithal replied, his eyes flickering with hope.

'His name is Wali, isn't it?' Bachal asked.

'It is. It is, sir,' Jannu replied eagerly.

'Hmm.' Bachal was pensive for a few moments, Jannu and Marvi waiting for his reply. 'You will get your son back, and soon,' he declared.

Marvi's expression changed completely as she was overtaken by his confidence and authority.

Thirty-three

Some of the water drained away and some was absorbed by the earth, heralding the end of the sojourn. People started to pack their bags, bracing for the return journey. They spent most of the last night gossiping with new-found friends and exchanging promises to stay in touch. They shared rope to tie their possessions and helped each other in doing so. Early next morning, the men helped their women place scuttles and baskets on their heads and heaved the heavier items onto their own backs. The children we asked to carry bottles of water and packets of biscuits and warned not to drink or eat without permission. After one last inspection of their temporary abodes, they set foot into the ankle-deep water and were on their way. The fathers walked in the lead and women and children queued up behind them. Different groups headed in different directions; some goading the animals they had managed to bring along. They told each other to walk faster as the distances were long. As they increased their speed, the children had to run every now and then to catch up with the adults. Walking on slippery mud, still submerged in murky water, was difficult, but they kept on plodding, happy to return home. Initially, an upbeat mood prevailed among the returning multitude. They talked excitedly as they walked. They had defied death when the water came and had run for their lives in chaos. Now, they laughed about it, relating stories of confusion. The escape became a conceivable event after they had successfully met the challenge, but their mood became sombre when their elders reminded them of the problems ahead. For a while, they thought of their washed-away houses and grain silos, the animals they could not rescue and the relatives who had gone missing. They could not escape thoughts of the carcasses that awaited them and the diseases that threatened their survival. Yet, they quickly returned to jest and laughter, telling themselves they would cross those bridges when they came to them.

The air was humid and acrid. The treacherous sun that had abandoned them on the day when dark clouds had vanquished the sky had now returned in full force. Nature refused to give them any reprieve, but they refused to give in. They rose and fell with remarkable fortitude. Those who reached their homes early got to work immediately, retrieving tin sheets that had been blown off their roofs and dragging logs and planks of wood that had floated away in the floodwater. They brought back broken tables and cots and sent their boys to look for the dogs and goats that they had failed to take along when they fled. They assessed the damage to their homes and made plans for repair.

Jannu and his family accompanied their community in the return journey. He had received a warm welcome on his arrival at the levee. His friends and relatives came to commiserate with him and shared their goods with him. Their attitude had greatly strengthened him. He had told Nooran about Bachal's promise to release their son from prison. Nooran was a different woman after she heard the news. She bragged about the return of her son to her relatives, confident that few would dare gossip about a girl whose brother was man enough to have killed another man. Still, she kept Marvi in a constant baleful gaze, watching her every step. Marvi remained indifferent towards her scrutiny, her eyes restlessly scanning the groups they overtook in the hope of catching a glimpse of Murad.

The people joked and laughed as they rebuilt their homes. They shared food and were not shy about asking for some if hungry. They remained generous despite their poverty. They raised their hands together in prayer and took care of the sick together. They grieved together and encouraged the fallen to rise, extending their hands for support. When such ingredients of human nature came together, new hamlets sprouted all over the delta within days. Life soon returned to normal and people got busy with their work. The fishermen returned to fishing and shopkeepers opened up shops. Farmers went to their farms and tillage. Herdsmen went in search of pastures to replenish their stocks. They didn't know that the worst was yet to come.

With the passage of time, memories of the cyclone had begun to fade and the challenges of its aftermath had begun to materialize. Disease took its toll, some died and others survived. Faced with the more pressing demands of survival, people didn't linger with funerals and mourning. They quickly returned to their workplaces to earn food for their families. It took the government a long time to start repair of the leaks in the canal, but the work was soon halted to await arrival of more experts. The government had kept up the charade of a large-scale relief effort, but people felt abandoned and alienated.

The worst fears of the people started to materialize, staring them in the face. The canal's water, replete with chemicals, started taking its toll. The resultant damage was more severe than the harm that slow underground seepage could have. Their earth had been poisoned. Inexorable and insidious damage to their lands continued. Trees still grew leaves, but the leaves were no more green and turgid. They appeared desiccated and frayed at the edges. The grass looked wilted and yellow. Wild cats found many dead crows and sparrows, which had dropped out of the sky. Sailboats trawled the lake but returned empty, the fishermen told stories of seeing dead fish floating in the water. The farmers were disappointed with their crops and took the matter to their co-operative society. Soil samples were sent for testing and the results indicated the presence of toxic chemicals in the soil and its hyper-salinity. The people cursed the canal for their miseries and were angered by the cold response from their government.

Thirty-four

Nooran had rarely brought their drinking water from the lake. She preferred a well almost a kilometre away because its water was cold and sweet. For years, she had regularly trekked to the well, finely balancing two pitchers on her head. Since their return from the levee, they drank bottled water for some time and then relied on the water from the lake to drink and to cook their meals. Lately, the lake's water had started to taste bitter, and so one day, Jannu wistfully mentioned the water from the well. The next day, Nooran placed two pitchers on her head and two on Marvi's head and headed for the well. Marvi hated carrying the pitchers, but this could be an opportunity for a chance meeting with Murad and she happily followed her mother.

The path to the well ran through green fields. They saw farmers busy with tillage. As they came close to one farmer transplanting tomato seedlings to his field, Nooran stopped.

'Are those tomatoes you are growing?' she asked the farmer.

'I can only hope my efforts will be rewarded,' the farmer replied, pleased to have a break.

'Why shouldn't you be rewarded?' Nooran asked. 'The floods are good for crops.'

'Yes, but it happens when the river floods. This time the water came from the sea,' he answered.

'The seawater came and went. It happened two months ago. Are you still concerned?' she said.

'It is not so simple, my sister,' the farmer remarked, and returned to his work.

When Nooran arrived at the well, she was disappointed to see only two women there. 'Where is everyone else?' she asked, looking at one of the women who had just ladled some water from the leather bucket and had quickly spat it out, contorting her features with distaste.

'What's wrong?' Nooran asked.

'The water is salty,' the woman replied.

Marvi stepped forward to taste the water and she too quickly spat it out. 'She is right,' Marvi told Nooran.

'How far is the next well?' Nooran asked the women.

'Two kilometres away near Deh Kamharam, I am going there if you want to come along,' the woman replied.

Deh Kamharam was Murad's village. Marvi prayed to heaven that her mother would agree to go but was disappointed when Nooran refused.

'I can go with her,' Marvi said excitedly.

'No. We will go home,' her mother snubbed her.

Marvi reluctantly followed when Nooran started walking back. It had been weeks since she last saw Murad and she was beginning to feel desperate.

'Let Wali come back and you will learn how to behave,' Nooran said, abruptly stopping and turning to look at her daughter in anger.

Marvi stayed silent, after a while muttering to herself, 'When my brother comes, he will take my side.' She was confident about her claim.

When they returned, they saw Mithal waiting for them on a cot under the tree. Nooran greeted him warmly, scanning the goods he had brought for them.

'I will make tea for him. You bring the sacks inside,' she told Marvi, and hurried indoors.

'So, how are you?' Mithal asked Marvi once Nooran was gone.

'I am barely alive. You made me a solemn promise,' she reminded Mithal.

'I have been thinking about it. You have not changed your mind?' Mithal asked her.

'Not in this life. I belong to Murad and this will never change,' she said in a steely tone. 'Never ever.'

Mithal thought to himself silently. 'I want this to happen in an acceptable manner,' he finally said.

'It was you who said Bachal will not let it happen that way,' Marvi was quick to remind him.

'I remember, but I will ask Murad to send his sister once and ask for your hand. I have yet to make arrangements for your stay in the city. A visit from his sister will satisfy my conscience,' he explained.

'Ask him. He will send his sister, but this will not make any difference. My mother hates Murad. She has forgotten that we are alive only because of him.' Marvi was in tears, and sat on the ground near Mithal's feet, joined her palms and poignantly begged, 'Help me. I cannot live without him.'

Mithal placed his hand on hers and turned his face away so that she wouldn't be able to see his tearful eyes. Nooran emerged from the house with a cup of steaming tea and Marvi quickly rose from the ground. She picked up the sacks Mithal had brought and stepped inside the house.

Thirty-five

People turned their heads in curiosity when a government-owned vehicle entered the small bazaar. The inside of the vehicle was not visible because of the dark tinted windows. Its tires were covered in dirt and the emblem on the side was only half visible under a layer of mud. The vehicle stopped near a shop and one of the windows slid down. The man in the driver's seat waved to a young man, who quickly came to the car. They talked for a while and then the shopkeeper called loudly to the others.

'Hey, we have guests from the government. They want to know if we have any problems.'

In no time, the vehicle was surrounded by an obstreperous crowd. The man behind the steering wheel didn't fail to sense the hostility of the people.

'I think we should move on,' a sepoy in the back seat whispered. A man in the passenger seat agreed.

'We have to find out. That is what we were sent to do. We are supposed to talk to people before we file our report,' the driver said.

'I don't think we are welcome,' the sepoy said, and before he had finished his sentence, someone smashed the car's rear windshield, causing him to quickly duck in fear. 'Go! For god's sake move,' he screamed.

Before the vehicle could move, people started to bombard it with sticks and stones. It was a narrow escape for the government officials. As the vehicle sped away, they heard people shouting profanities and threatening to kill them.

The event electrified village after village as the news spread. Saajan, who had been at the forefront of this attack, became a well-known name. People came to him to hear the story first hand and praised him for his boldness. Within a few days, his face became the face of the contempt people had developed against their representatives.

Saajan was happy at this transformation from anonymity to popularity as an anarchist daredevil. What he didn't know was that the innocuous policeman in the back seat had seen his face and heard his name many times. A complaint was subsequently lodged in the area police station against him, but he wasn't arrested despite the fact that the police knew of his shop and his home very well. It seemed this single event had proved a milestone in an uprising by the people of the delta. The movement gained momentum as more villagers rallied to the bazaar and Saajan spoke to them. They were unanimous in blaming the government for not listening to them when they had spoken out against the canal two years ago. They bitterly criticized the politicians for executing the project for their personal gain and for allowing contractors to use substandard materials and bypass the necessary precautionary measures they had promised.

'We want compensation for what the canal has done to us. The government must compensate every family,' Saajan said, repeating his message until it became the cry of the day.

~

Murad dropped the load of dry grass and tinder near the kiln and sat down for some rest. He looked at Athee who was busy throwing yet more pots.

'Why are we toiling, Athee? No one has money to buy our pots,' he said.

'Don't lose heart. They will come in droves once they receive compensation from the government,' Athee replied.

'Hah! It has been just two days since people started talking of compensation and you are already optimistic! The government will never agree to what the people are asking for.' He got up and started layering the pit with dry grass and tinder to bake the pots.

'Well, the politicians will have to do something if they want our votes next time,' Athee commented.

'They'll do "something", Athee. They will definitely do "something".'

'What?' she asked.

'Steal our money. That is the only thing they are good at,' Murad replied, still busy with the kiln.

Athee laughed at his manner of blaming the politicians but nodded her head in agreement.

'We deserve our fate,' he said bitterly, placing pots over the bed he had prepared.

As he fumbled in his pocket for the matchbox, he heard a motorcycle come to a stop in front of their door. Someone called his name and Murad briskly walked to the door, knowing well who the visitor was.

'Will you bring him in?' Athee asked.

'No. I will take him to Bakhshoo's cafe,' Murad replied as he reached the door. He opened it and saw Mithal waiting for him. 'I knew it was you,' he said, warmly shaking his hand. 'Let's go and have a cold drink.'

Mithal drove them to the cafe, which was only five minutes away, and took a chair while Murad went to fetch drinks.

'How are things with you?' Mithal asked once he had returned.

'Not good. I am waiting for you to make good on your promise,' he replied. 'The promise a father made to his daughter!'

'I remember my promise and I am working on it. Such things take time. People lose their lives in such matters. That life might be yours or mine. Perhaps both of ours,' he said in a serious tone.

'I know, and I am prepared for it,' Murad replied in an equally serious voice.

Mithal raised his eyebrows in surprise. 'You would die for her?' he asked.

'And more. If there was more,' Murad said, looking him straight in the eyes.

Mithal kept silent, searching his face for a sign of falsehood. He didn't find any. Murad was earnest in what he said.

'And I could take a life too. I wish someone would warn Bachal,' Murad added, grinding his teeth.

'He can offer you a lot of money, an amount beyond your dreams,' Mithal said, continuing to test the iron in his words.

'I spit on his money.' Murad contorted his face in spite.

'More than you will ever earn in your life.' Mithal smiled.

'I still spit on it,' Murad said with the same vehemence.

Mithal was silent for a long time, deep in thought, prominent creases appearing on his forehead as he focused his vision on the bottle of cold drink sitting in front of him. 'Okay, my dear boy. I stand by my promise, but don't do anything foolish before then,' he said finally.

Murad heaved a sigh of relief. Mithal picked the bottle up to drink whatever remained.

Thirty-six

Throngs of people arrived on the road that connected the port city to the many cities inland. Most of them were able-bodied young men fuming with anger. It was the start of the day. Many trucks and trawlers were speeding towards their destinations, most carrying goods from the port. The crowd was chanting slogans for compensation in one voice. With clenched fists and angry faces, they swarmed the road. Saajan arrived and people gathered around him. He raised his hand and the crowds fell silent to listen to him.

'Don't let the traffic through. Block the road,' he commanded.

People hurriedly picked large stones and placed them on the road. Some squatted down in the middle of the road and others ran towards moving vehicles and pelted them with rocks. A truck veered away from the approaching crowd and overturned in the process. People rushed forward, dragged the driver out and began beating him. Many others could be seen running towards the road to join the melee. Traffic stopped on both sides and a queue formed, tailing back for a kilometre. Saajan grabbed a loudspeaker and started addressing the crowd. The more he spoke, the more frenzied the crowd became. Groups of youth damaged electricity poles and sign boards. Dissatisfied, they ran to the truck and set it on fire. The sound of police sirens rose over the cacophony. Saajan screamed into the loudspeaker.

'Stay and face them,' he commanded.

The police arrived and rushed toward the crowds, waving their batons and firing tear-gas shells. The crowd fought back with sticks and stones, inflicting injury for injury, drawing blood for blood and the fracas continued for some time. It ended only once reinforcements arrived to support the beleaguered policemen. People scattered away into fields and the police failed to arrest anyone. The boulders and other obstacles were removed from the road and it was opened for traffic. Saajan left the scene on his motorcycle, driving down a small dirt path skirting the fields on the far side of the highway, delighted at the impact he had made.

A few days after this incident, Nooran was sitting on a cot under the tree. It was early morning and the heath was blanketed in thick fog. She had left Marvi to her daily chores and could hear her chopping wood in the nearby thicket. Jannu was still inside the house, finishing his tea and silently mourning the loss of his hand. It appeared as though people had not yet left their homes for work. Apart from the movement of stray dogs, life was at a standstill. Absent-mindedly watching the scene, she did not see Marvi come out of the thicket with a load of wood on her head. The girl stopped by Nooran and stood still, peering into the fog.

'Someone is coming!' she announced in a hoarse whisper.

Nooran, suddenly aware of her presence, briskly turned to look at her and then followed her gaze to see a human figure lurking in the haze.

'Wali?' Nooran gasped. They both waited in silence, eyes fixed on the approaching person.

'Call your father,' Nooran managed to say, her mouth going dry at the rush of adrenaline.

'Baba,' Marvi was quick to shout, and a few moments later her father came out running.

'Look!' Nooran pointed in the direction of the figure slowly making its way towards them.

Jannu squinted at it, holding his breath. Torturous moments passed before his gait became discernable.

'Wali?!' Jannu said.

The three of them stood paralysed, oscillating between hope and doubt. Then they saw him wave both his arms and they darted in his direction. Marvi was in the lead, leaping like a deer in flight. Jannu was some distance behind and Nooran behind him shouting at them to wait for her. Marvi reached him first and screamed with joy.

'It is Wali, my brother!' She hugged him and kissed him on his face and hands while Wali laughed.

Jannu arrived after her and embraced him. Nooran held him in a tight hug for the longest time, crying with disbelief and joy. Then, they started to walk back to their home in absolute bliss, Jannu and Nooran flanking him with Marvi frolicking in front.

'You have grown into a strong man, brother,' she said, looking at him admiringly.

'He is tall like me,' Jannu was quick to add.

As he extended his right hand to touch him, Wali noticed the amputation stump. His eyes became wet as he looked at his father. 'I cried when Mithal told me, but don't worry, baba, I am your right hand,' Wali said solemnly.

'You sure are,' Jannu said, refusing to be melancholic in this moment of joy.

'I will take care of you now. I am a fully-trained mechanic and a driver now!' Wali revealed with pride.

'Oh, you are?' All of them were surprised.

'Yes. I learned the art in jail. My teacher was very fond of me because I relieved him of most of his work,' he said, puffing his chest.

They sat around the hearth after reaching the house and Nooran got busy with making breakfast for her son. Marvi kept looking at him and Jannu kissed him again and again.

'Did you meet Bachal?' Jannu asked suddenly.

'Yes, I did. Mithal took me to see him. Bachal is a very kind and powerful man. He gave you back your son, baba,' he said with total reverence in his voice. 'Otherwise, I would have rotted in jail forever.'

'We can't thank him enough.' Jannu nodded his head in agreement.

'So, what are your plans?' Marvi asked to change the subject.

'I wish I had money. I want to set up a workshop in a city,' Wali replied. He looked around and added, 'We could leave this desolate land for good.'

Jannu smiled mildly. 'I didn't want to leave my home. I left it once and see what happened to me? The shelter of one's own home is a great blessing. It saves you from many a humiliation. These walls protect you from peering eyes and guard your modesty,' he said in a serious tone. 'I have a grown-up daughter to take care of.'

'I walked a long distance here and saw what has happened to these lands. It was hard to find drinking water, baba,' Wali replied. 'The crops are weak and there is no grass left.'

'You can talk about it later. Don't spoil my joy,' Nooran rebuked

Jannu, placing bread and a fried egg in front of Wali, who didn't wait to break bread.

After the breakfast, Marvi held his hand and dragged him towards the door. 'Come and I will tell you about the three scary nights we spent in the tree. Your hammock was of great use during that time.'

She was eager to introduce him to Murad and needed to be alone with him. They stepped out of the house and walked to the tree.

'It was horrible, Wali. The tree was cocooned in spider webs. There were hundreds of those wretched creatures all around us and the water was chest-high as far as we could see. We sat here, hungry and thirsty, during the day and the night until he came.' Her voice changed and her eyes became dreamy.

'I know the whole story,' Wali said with disinterest. 'Mithal told me. He is a talkative man.'

'Did he tell you about Murad?' Marvi asked timidly.

'He did.'

Wali's reply was flat and brief. Marvi felt awkward at his coldness and was relieved when she heard Nooran call out to her. She rushed back towards the house.

Thirty-seven

The police officer in charge of the area police station stood with his head bent and eyes fixed on the plush carpet that covered the floor from wall to wall. He was in the presence of the minister for internal affairs. This was an overwhelming moment in his life. Next to the minister sat Bachal, another politician of great prominence. The police officer felt small and guilty without reason.

'I feel as though you don't want to keep your job,' the minister barked, and the officer could not help but think of his two schoolgoing daughters.

'I do want to, sir,' he managed to whimper.

"Then how come this boy Saajan is still at large despite engineering the sit-in on the highway and fighting the police force?' the minister roared.

'We will apprehend him soon, sir,' the policeman replied.

'Apprehend?! That is all you will do?' the minister asked.

'Whatever you order, sir,' the policeman said.

'Nip the evil in the bud! Do you understand? Nip the evil in the bud. Once and for all.' The minister's anger was mounting. 'And there is more. This boy is not alone. He has an accomplice;

the brains behind all of this,' the minister said, and struggling to remember the name of the accomplice, snapped his fingers to jog his memory.

'Murad,' Bachal finished for him. 'Of Deh Kamharam.'

'Yes, Murad of Deh Kamharam,' the minister repeated vehemently. 'You have two names now, go and do something.'

The minister rudely waved his hand in dismissal. The officer saluted with zeal and exited the office.

On his long drive back to the police station, he brooded over the two names he had been ordered to take care of. He knew about Saajan very well, but the second name puzzled him. He was well aware of the people associated with crime in his territory but had never heard his name before. But having been told that Murad was from Deh Kamharam, finding him would be a cinch. His orders were unambiguous, and though he had personal limits, they stretched far outside the boundaries of the law. He decided to make inquiries before following his orders.

The persistent banging on the door woke Athee. She sat up in bed, surprised at this visitor so late in the night. Slipping her feet into her shoes, she grabbed her gun and hid it under her shawl. She walked to the door and opened it to find a stranger, his face half covered by a scarf. Athee's grip on the gun tightened.

'Is this Murad's house?' the visitor asked in a hushed voice.

'It is,' Athee replied.

'I have been sent by someone who wishes you well. If you are Athee, the potter...' He stopped, raising his eyebrows enquiringly.

Athee nodded her head in an affirmative and the visitor spoke again.

'Someone very powerful is bent on taking his life.'

'Why should I believe you?' Athee asked, suddenly shaken at the thought of this anonymous enemy.

'Because you will gain nothing by risking Murad's life,' the visitor said.

'Who is our enemy? What is his name?' Athee asked nervously.

'I can't give you names. Send him away to some place where no one will come looking for him,' the stranger said and briskly walked away.

Athee's grip on the gun had loosened due to the sweat on her palms. She closed the door and returned to the courtyard, where she sat down to think. Murad was precious to her, a gateway to whatever happiness her life had to offer. She wanted him to marry and have children for her to raise. She had imagined them running around in her courtyard and smiled at the thought of their laughter. Without Murad, the emptiness of her life was too dreadful to bear thinking about. She made a decision and rushed to his room to wake him up.

After the final meeting with the boys, who had invited him for a discussion about the movement for compensation, Saajan was ready to return home. It was dangerous to travel long distances during the night in that area but the intrepid Saajan refused to be cowed by the mention of robbers. He checked his revolver and tucked it into the belt of his trousers for easy access. Then, he kick-started his motorcycle and moved on as his hosts waved him goodbye. Soon, the red taillight of his vehicle was invisible to them.

Night in the wilderness brings with it mysteries that threaten the safety of those who dare to brave it. Saajan was used to these presumed and real dangers and he drove on, occupied with thoughts of the protest they had planned. The headlights of the motorcycle were too dim, and he was finding it difficult to keep his vehicle on the bumpy dirt track, and so he failed to see the people waiting for him near the grove of trees. By the time he saw them, it was too late. Something struck him and he fell, his motorcycle veering away into the bush. He was quick to draw his gun despite the fall, but as its metal glinted in the light of the stars, one of his adversaries fired his weapon. The sound of the gunshot was followed by a startled frenzy of birds' wings and silence quickly returned. Both the motorcycle and its rider were dragged to the pickup truck and it rolled forward without turning on its headlights.

Thirty-eight

The elders of the fishermen's community gathered to discuss a strategy for survival in the face of an increasing paucity of fish. Jannu brought Wali along with him. After all, he was more enlightened than the others because of his knowledge of car machines, his time in jail and a murder to his credit. He was warmly received and given a place of prominence. After the initial exchange of pleasantries, their conversation focused on the living conditions in the languishing delta.

'It has become so hard to find drinking water, let alone food to eat,' Moti lamented.

'I fail to understand why the wells have turned salty,' an exasperated Mehar said.

'It happens when the sea enters a river through its mouth and travels for a significant distance. Its saline water seeps through the bed of the river and mixes with the underground water. That is how the wells turn salty,' an elder explained.

'How long is it going to stay that way?' Moti asked.

'No one knows,' the elder replied.

'No water to drink. No food to feed our children. No wonder

many people have left,' another man said.

'The herders have already moved on. Their animals were dying because of the contaminated water they drank,' someone remarked.

'There is no alternative. We will also have to go,' Mehar added.

'Go where?' Jannu protested. 'No paradise awaits us beyond this land, where our forefathers lived. Do you want to become homeless and spend your nights on roadsides, begging during the day?' he spoke persistently, looking at their faces for a reply to the questions he posed.

'It is a long coast, Jannu. There are many villages inhabited by our brothers. I am sure we can find employment if we leave,' an equally passionate Ghulam said.

This did not impress Jannu. He persisted in his appeal against migration. 'We should stay put. Better days will come.'

'You can stay put, Jannu, because you have a rich man as a friend. We don't even have stale bread to eat,' one of his cousins reminded Jannu, and he squirmed at the barb. The general mood of hopelessness, it seemed, was prevailing.

'He is my friend because I did him favours.' Jannu was quick to offer an explanation though no one had asked for it. 'He stayed at my place, ate my food and used my boat to hunt geese,' he quickly added to kill any presumptions.

'Yes! Goose hunting!' another villager remarked meaningfully.

'I have decided to leave,' Moti announced, and Jannu was relieved at the change of subject. Many others agreed with him and Jannu was shocked at the majority's intention to emigrate. People got up to leave but Jannu persisted in trying to change their minds.

'The government will come to our aid. It will give us money to remake our boats and do something about the salt in the water,' he proclaimed, but few were prepared to pay him heed.

'Compensation money?! Do you know what happened to the boy who was leading the struggle for compensation?' one man asked him. 'He has disappeared. There is no trace of him. That is what happens to people who make trouble for the government. Don't give us false hope.'

Another fisherman, and then another, derided him and left the meeting place. Soon, the place was empty.

On their way back, Jannu and Wali walked in silence, both submerged in their own thoughts.

'Why are you so opposed to emigration?' Wali finally decided to reopen the subject with his father.

Wali had his owns dreams to pursue. The wilderness was beginning to haunt him. It had the potential to bury his dreams. He wanted to start a repair workshop of his own, earn money and enjoy the comforts of an urban life. Jannu's obstinacy was beginning to annoy him.

'Because of your sister!' Jannu replied.

'What has she got to do with it?' Wali asked in surprise.

'The honour of a family depends on the conduct of its women. Especially those who are young,' he said.

'So?' Wali still didn't understand.

'If I lose the protection of my house and take to the road in a strange place, I will be at the mercy of strangers and their prying eyes. They will try to approach her in many guises and cheat us out of the only asset we have—our honour. I had a taste of it during the days I spent in the hospital and on the levee,' Jannu explained. 'I know there is nothing left to enable me to earn a living, but better to be poor than dishonoured. I would have left if I had a home to live in the city I migrate to.'

'Why don't you marry her off?' Wali could see the weight of his argument.

'Your mother talked to her about this, but she refused.' Wali sighed.

'She had the gall to refuse?' Wali could not believe his ears.

'Wake up to reality, Wali. She is no more the timid girl you knew. She transcended her years during the days of hardship we faced. I have to say, she fought valiantly for our lives, but the experience changed her completely. She can now look you in the eyes and say what she wants to.'

Wali listened in disbelief and was quiet when his father stopped talking.

'There is more,' Jannu said, and Wali looked at him expectantly. 'This boy who came to rescue us on the third night has possessed her since then. It is only him she will agree to marry.'

Wali was shocked to hear of this sentiment his sister had nurtured. This was something of which he could never approve. 'Why don't you beat her out of this shameful behaviour?' He was furious.

'There would be no gain,' Jannu said. 'It wouldn't work. She will not forget about the boy even if you hold a dagger to her throat.'

'How can you be so sure?' Wali asked, still seething with anger.

Jannu smiled bitterly. 'I am an old man, Wali. I have seen enough of the world to know a few things.'

'Why don't you wed her to this boy then?' Wali asked.

'That will be a proof of our complicity in this dishonourable relationship. People already have their doubts and talk about it. I cannot agree to the proposal. That is my predicament,' Jannu replied.

Thirty-nine

Groups of young men covered every nook and corner of the sprawling region in search of Saajan. They didn't find any clues to his whereabouts. They talked to his friends and relatives in all the villages near and far in their futile efforts. Many of them were leery of the police, they had heard of many people who had died in police custody and they blamed them for his disappearance. A group was sent to the police station to make inquiries. The boys did not hide their anger when they confronted the officer in charge. They asked for a meeting with Saajan, but the police denied any knowledge of him. They were invited to look through the lockup for their own satisfaction. Two boys went to search for him in the lockup, but returned disappointed. They threatened the officer in charge with dire consequences if the police were discovered to have a role in his disappearance. The officer managed to keep his cool during the altercation, but heaved a sigh of relief when they exited his office, still shouting profanities. The mob headed for the gate and a few strayed toward the abandoned vehicles heaped on top of each other in a corner. They saw many vehicles of different types that had been impounded during police actions and never returned to their owners. As the boys shifted through the pile of gutted and dismantled vehicles, one of the boys cried out.

'Look!'

He was pointing towards the relatively fresh skeleton of a gutted motorcycle with three rear-view mirrors on its handle.

'Saajan had an extra mirror fixed to the handlebar,' he exclaimed.

Others joined him to inspect it and they quickly ascertained that it had been Saajan's motorcycle.

'Let us go back and talk to them,' one of them suggested in anger.

'No, we will come back later. We will come prepared,' their leader declared, and asked them to leave.

Two policemen stood on the veranda observing the boys inspecting the freshly gutted skeleton of Saajan's motorcycle.

'I think they know. I will go and tell the boss,' one said, and briskly walked towards the officer in charge.

He knew the matter wouldn't end there.

~

By sunrise the next day, young men had come together to march towards the police station, gaining in strength as they passed each village along the way. Having covered a few kilometres in distance, the crowd had swollen to several hundred. They were armed with sticks, stones and petrol bombs and chanted slogans of vengeance in unison. The crowd increased its speed when the police station was in sight, their voices booming across the fields and houses.

The people in the village and the bazaar heard the chanting and scrambled to the rooftops to see the crowd approaching like a swarm of locusts. Shopkeepers hurriedly pulled down shutters and women dragged their children home in panic. Street vendors nervously pushed their carts away from the crowd's path. Doors were banged shut and latched.

'Shut the gate and grab your weapons,' the officer in charge came screaming down the stairs.

A flurry of activity brought the police force to life.

'I want five people on the rooftops ready to fire if we lose control,' he yelled as he hurried into his office.

He picked up the phone and started dialing numbers with trembling hands, shouting into the mouthpiece for help. The crowd arrived at the police station and started pelting it with stones. A group ran to the gate and started pushing it open. Two policemen were hit with stones and blood gushed from the wounds on their foreheads. A petrol bomb crashed into the heap of abandoned vehicles and flames leaped skywards. The police fired a volley into the air and retaliated with tear-gas shells, but the pelting intensified. The main gate creaked against the weight of the mob pushing against it. As more petrol bombs were hurled into the compound, a policeman caught fire and fell to the ground, rolling in agony. Two men darted forward to throw a blanket over him and then dragged him into one of the rooms. The officer in charge shouted orders to fire into the crowd. A few guns rattled and two of the protestors were hit. This caused a brief pause in the pelting of stones, but it picked up with renewed intensity as the shock of the gunfire was met with renewed anger. The helpless officer in charge ran from the compound to the rooftop and back. His tear-gas shells had all been fired and the gate would give way at any moment. He ordered again for his men to fire into the mob at the gate and his subordinates obeyed, injuring more people. This time the protesters scurried to take shelter and it was then that the fast approaching sound of police vehicles became audible. A few men rushed towards the building once more, throwing more petrol bombs that caused the building to catch fire. As thick smoke started billowing from the blaze, the first rescue force arrived. Seeing them, the crowd made a hasty retreat. Men spread out in different directions, leaving behind the injured and the dead.

Forty

During the ensuing days, hundreds of policemen inundated the villages, making arrest after arrest. The government invited a few elders to talks and pacified them with threats and bribes. They returned to their villages and subdued whatever unrest there was. With Saajan's disappearance and the purchase of their loyalty, the uprising was vanquished and people quietly gave up their claims to compensation. The fishermen around the lake started migrating. Jannu watched families leave on camel carts and hired trucks as he stubbornly stayed behind in defence of his honour. The more pragmatic Wali bragged about his expertise as a mechanic and continued to stress to his father that better days would follow their initial suffering if they moved. Mithal visited regularly with food for the family in the tractor.

'This is a wonderful piece of machinery,' Wali said to his father one day. 'The trolley is spacious, wide enough for our family to cook and sleep in. It is like a home on wheels.'

Jannu peeped into the trolley and nodded his head in agreement. 'It is spacious,' he remarked. 'But what if it rains?'

'I can fix a canopy over it in half an hour,' Wali replied. 'If we had this tractor, we could place all our possessions in it and still have enough room to lie down or recline, driving across villages and from one city to another, enjoying the ride.'

Jannu walked around the tractor nodding as Wali's wistful words drove his point home. 'I wish we had this. If we did, I would agree to migrate today,' Jannu finally announced. 'Would you be able to place curtains on the side to keep the women protected from strangers?' he asked.

'Of course,' Wali reassured him. 'But it is not ours and we will never possess one.'

'It can be yours if you want!'

Both of them jumped in surprise at Mithal's remark, wondering when he had arrived.

'Don't make fun of us, Mithal. We are poor people,' Jannu said sheepishly.

Mithal stopped grinning and his expression changed. 'I am serious, Jannu,' he said plainly.

'How?' Wali was quick to ask.

'I will tell you before I leave' Mithal said. 'Now go and send Marvi with a hot cup of tea so that I can be on my way,' he said authoritatively, dismissing them both.

After a few minutes, Marvi emerged with his tea. Mithal took the cup of tea from her and then looked around to make sure that the men had gone.

'Sit down,' he told Marvi.

She sat down and looked at him. 'What is it?' she asked.

'I want to ask you one final time. Do you still stand by your decision to wed Murad and no one else?' he asked.

'Never doubt it,' she replied, her features taking a steely expression.

'Now listen to me carefully. I will ask his sister to visit your parents and ask for your hand. I will also pressure your parents to the best of my ability. But what if they refuse?' he asked.

'Let this happen first. I will see after their refusal,' Marvi answered.

'Bachal is going to propose to you too. He has asked me to give his message to your father. I have not done that as yet, but I dare not postpone it much longer. I don't think Jannu is any longer in a position to refuse all that which he is offering in return,' he told Marvi.

'In that case, I will be left with no option but to leave. Bachal will never have me alive,' she declared coldly. 'Do you remember what you swore to me?' she asked, looking straight into his eyes.

Mithal did not waver. 'I stand by my promise. I have already arranged a place for the two of you to stay in the port city. I will take you there personally. Are you prepared to take this risk? You know it is an issue of honour.'

'I know, but I will do it if there is no alternative. I am prepared to take the risk.' She sounded clear-headed and decisive.

'Okay. If worst comes to worst and this remains the only choice, then I will tell you how and when. I hope you trust me without a shadow of doubt.'

'We trust you,' Marvi replied.

Forty-one

Murad had spent a week at a distant aunt's house and every minute of his incarceration had been an agony. He heard stories of agitation and death back home and was greatly saddened. He felt ensnared. He had agreed to hide because Athee asked him to, but it was against his temperament. When at home, he had often gone to the lake hoping for a chance meeting with Marvi. Now he was thirty-two kilometres away from the lake, and he was not allowed to leave the house. His frustration mounted with every passing day. So, when Athee arrived much earlier than he expected, he was overjoyed.

'You have come to take me home, haven't you?' he asked excitedly.

She was as happy as he was. 'Hop on and I will take you home,' she said.

'What about the threat?' he asked.

'I don't think it was real. Someone had connected you with Saajan to the police. Now they are embroiled in a more serious problem of their own and they cannot be bothered with you,' she said.

Murad took the pillion seat and Athee drove on. 'Where did you get the motorcycle?' Murad asked.

'I borrowed it from the cafe owner,' she screamed over the sound of the engine and the wind.

They arrived home after an hour. Murad saw a new latch on the door and noticed Athee take her gun out of some deep pocket in her shirt. He could not help but smile at her daring. She was prepared for anything.

'There is something else I am going to do for you,' she told Murad.

'What, Athee?' he asked.

'Tomorrow I will go to Jannu's place and ask for Marvi's hand in marriage for you,' she said.

Murad smiled and hugged her tightly.

The sound of the approaching motorcycle attracted Marvi's attention. She dropped her broom and came out of the house to see who it was. She expected to see a man but was surprised to find a flowing green shawl fluttering in the wind. A broad smile came to her lips when she recognized the rider as Athee. She ran forward to welcome her. They hugged and kissed each other with great warmth. Holding hands, they walked towards the house.

'Is your father home?' Athee asked her.

'No, but he will return soon. Any minute now,' Marvi replied.

'How are you?' Athee stopped, scanned her face and asked in a concerned tone.

'I don't know, Athee. Sometimes I feel I am still trapped in the tree with spiders spinning webs around me,' she said sadly.

'Don't worry. I am here to ask for your hand for my brother.

We will take you away and you will live like the queen that you are,' Athee teased her.

Marvi blushed and covered her face with her hands.

'Take me to your mother,' Athee said, and took her arm.

Nooran's expression hardened the moment she saw Athee enter the house with Marvi by her side. Athee's buoyant greeting did little to return warmth to her face. She reluctantly invited Athee to sit. Marvi went to the heath.

'I will make tea for you,' she said, but she focused her attention on the conversation her mother was having with their guest.

'Jannu is not home. You should have informed us before coming,' Nooran said.

'Marvi told me he will be arriving soon.' Athee wanted the conversation to continue. 'Has he gone for work?' she asked.

'He does not go for any work. Don't you know his hand was chopped off when your brother took him to the hospital?' Nooran said bitterly.

'He would have lost his life if the hand had not been amputated. This is what the doctor told them,' Athee said defensively.

'That is a lie your brother told. He crippled my husband and lured my innocent daughter.' Nooran had raised her voice, at which point Marvi decided to intervene, waving a finger in her mother's face.

'Don't blame her,' she said. 'It was my decision to give permission to the doctor. You should remember that it was her brother who rescued us all from death when we were trapped in this tree.'

Athee was at a loss for words at this unexpected flare-up. She furtively gestured to Marvi to stay calm. 'Bring my tea, darling,' she said.

'Aren't you afraid of your brother when you say things in defence of another man?' Nooran rebuked Marvi who was quick to retort.

'I vanquished my fear in the three nights we spent in the tree while I nursed baba and dripped water in your mouth. You owe me your life, mother,' she stressed.

Athee could only sit silently during the altercation, ruing her arrival while Jannu was away. Nooran turned her face away, refusing to talk to Athee. Thankfully, Jannu entered the house and stood there wondering who their visitor was.

'This is the sister of the boy who took you to the hospital,' Nooran rudely introduced her.

'I see. Please drink your tea. It is getting cold.' He was more hospitable than Nooran. An awkward silence followed as he sat down across from their guest.

'You know Murad, don't you?' Athee addressed him.

'I do vaguely remember his face. What about him?' Jannu replied.

'He is a good-looking, sincere young man. He is a seasoned potter too. He can earn a good living to support a family,' Athee said.

'I am sure he is.' Jannu remained unimpressed and detached.

'I have come to ask you for something on his behalf.' Athee spread her shawl in the way that beggars do.

'What can I give you?! I am a poor cripple myself,' Jannu said with some self-pity.

'You possess the treasure I have come to beg you for. Give us Marvi and we will be your vassals for life,' Athee beseeched him.

Jannu glanced at his wife's frowning face and then fixed his gaze upon the floor. He remained silent for a long time as Athee waited for his reply. Finally, he raised his head. 'Give me time to think,' he said in a serious tone.

Athee was glad to hear this. She had not expected more in her first meeting with the family. She thanked him profusely and asked when he wanted her to come again.

'In a week, perhaps,' Jannu replied.

'I will, brother Jannu. Please don't refuse,' Athee pleaded and took permission to leave.

Jannu saw her off at the door. Athee was smiling when the door closed behind her. What had started as a disaster had ended better than she had expected. She couldn't have asked for more. Of course, a father would need time to think before deciding upon his daughter's future, she thought. As she turned the corner of the house, she saw a man standing near her motorcycle.

'Are you the famous Athee?' the man asked when she came closer. The question brought a smile to her lips.

'How do you know me?' she asked.

'You know me too. I am Mithal,' the man said.

'Of course, I know you. You are a friend of Murad's,' Athee was excited to meet him.

'So, what did they say?' Mithal surprised her with his question.

'Say? About what?' she asked.

In response, Mithal smiled meaningfully and said, 'About giving their daughter to Murad in marriage.'

'You are as clever a man as I had figured,' Athee acknowledged. 'I think they will agree.'

'I will pray for your success.' Mithal waved his hand as she kick-started her motorcycle. 'You are women to reckon with. Someone told me you always carry a gun?'

Athee took a deep breath and nodded her head. 'Yes, I do.'

'The same someone told me that many years ago you stabbed a thief to death?' Mithal asked again.

'That's true,' Athee replied.

'Aren't you afraid you may die if you carry arms and are prepared to use them?' Mithal asked.

'One needs to be prepared to die if one wants to live.' She flashed her white teeth in a wide grin and shifted the gear to drive off. Mithal watched her for as long as she was visible, admiring her courage.

'You know her?' He heard Jannu ask and jerked his head around to face him.

'I hope I do,' Mithal said, and sat down on the cot.

'Did you walk here? I don't see your tractor,' Jannu said.

'I brought the tractor, but Wali took it. He has gone to see some friends,' Mithal answered.

Jannu shook his head. 'This boy would give his life for that tractor. He never stops talking about it.' He called out to Marvi to bring tea for Mithal.

'He does not have to give his life for the tractor. There is a better way,' Mithal remarked.

This was the second time Mithal had made the offer, but he stopped short of elaborating. Jannu was silent, musing over Mithal's statement. He didn't have to think very long. Mithal made the offer soon enough.

'I have brought you a special message from my master Bachal,' Mithal said, grabbing him to sit him down.

Jannu's heart skipped a beat and then raced like a wild deer. He sat down close to Mithal whose offer was candid and plain.

'Bachal wants to marry your daughter Marvi,' he said.

Jannu was stunned. He didn't know what to say. He stood up and slowly walked towards his home with his head bent. Marvi emerged from the house with a cup of tea for Mithal. She stopped briefly to look at her dazed father and then walked over to Mithal to give him the tea.

'Is something wrong?' she asked, gesturing towards Jannu.

Mithal shrugged his shoulders and took the hot cup of tea from her. 'Nothing that I know of.'

Forty-two

Before Mithal finished his tea, Wali had returned with the tractor. The brief drive had exhilarated him, and he came walking towards Mithal with a swagger, swinging the key chain around his index finger.

'How did it feel?' Mithal asked as he took the keys back.

'It was great,' Wali replied as he helped Mithal take the driver's seat.

'Do something to make it yours,' Mithal said, then waved and pressed the accelerator, throwing up a cloud of dust as he drove away.

Wali was left wondering about his cryptic message and stood there in silence for a moment before walking towards the house. It was quickly becoming dark. Jannu had just started eating his dinner when he entered. He washed his hands and joined him by the hearth. Marvi had already gone to the room to sleep. Nooran was sitting by the hearth, feeding the fire with twigs to keep it burning.

'Where have you been?' Jannu asked.

'I went all around the lake, from village to village, looking for anyone to talk to. I didn't find a single person. People have abandoned their homes and gone. The houses are empty, the doors are open and all I could see were stray dogs sniffing for food,' he replied.

'I know,' Jannu remarked flatly.

'I don't blame them for leaving the land of their forefathers. There is no food or water, just these precarious huts of straw and grass, foul air to breathe and eerie nights to live through. The prison was better!' Wali sounded frustrated and angry.

'What is there to do, Wali? This is our destiny,' Jannu said, but this only riled his son further.

'It is our destiny because you don't want to do anything to change it. You have given up, baba. You refuse to do anything, and you don't let me do something either. We are left alone in this desolation, surviving on the grains that Mithal brings. I could have earned a decent living if you had agreed to come with me to a city.' Wali was losing his temper.

'Why don't you tell him?' Nooran asked Jannu.

'Tell me what?' Wali asked his mother.

'There are two proposals for Marvi,' Nooran told him.

'Well, that is great! What have you decided?' Wali asked.

'We were waiting for you to help us make a decision,' Nooran said.

'Tell me, then,' Wali said eagerly.

'One is from Murad.' She couldn't hide the contempt in her voice.

'And the second?' Wali was getting restless.

'Bachal, the landlord,' Nooran revealed to his joy. Now he understood Mithal's departing message.

'I presume Bachal will give us his tractor and much more,' he said enquiringly.

Both Jannu and Nooran nodded their heads in agreement.

'Forget about Murad. He is just a flute-playing pauper. Agree to Bachal's proposal and you will have a rich son-in-law.' He could hardly suppress his excitement.

'A son-in-law ten years older than his father-in-law,' Jannu said bitingly.

'Forget his age. Look at the way our lives are going to change. The tractor is worth at least fifteen lakhs. We can sell it and buy a house and I can start a garage. What are you waiting for?' His voice rose with his excitement, all three of them oblivious of the girl standing behind them, listening to every word they said.

'You want to trade me for a tractor, my dear brother?'

They jumped at the sound of her voice but didn't dare turn and look her in the eye.

'I cried for you every single day when you were in prison and this is what you give me in return?' she said, sobbing, and ran back to the room.

They sat silently for a long time. Nooran broke the silence. 'She will not agree to another proposal while Murad is alive,' she said.

'She will have to. This is a matter of honour,' Wali said angrily and then got up. 'I will see to it.'

Forty-three

Mithal came to Deh Kamharam to see Murad, who was pleased to welcome him and took him to the cafe for cold drinks and sweets.

'So, what are we celebrating?' Mithal asked as he placed a large piece of the delicious sweets in his mouth.

'You know, Mithal. Athee told me she met you,' Murad replied.

'That is only one part of the story. She didn't say much when we met. Tell me how Marvi's parents reacted to your proposal. Does she feel they will agree?' Mithal asked.

'They will,' he said.

'What are your plans if they do?' Mithal asked.

'Marriage as soon as possible and then off we go,' Murad said to the other man's surprise.

'Go? Where?' he asked.

'Some place where we can earn a living. Haven't you noticed that many families have already migrated?' Murad replied.

Mithal ignored the subject of migration. 'What if they refuse?'

'That would be tragic,' Murad said, saddening visibly.

'What will you do in that case? This is the real question that you cannot avoid,' Mithal emphasized.

A dark shadow came over Murad's face. He looked at Mithal, trying to read the message he was trying to convey. 'Do you have any information for me?' he finally asked, his heart beating in anticipation.

'Yes, I do. They asked me to deliver this letter to your sister. It was dictated in front of me by Jannu. Wali wrote it. So, I know what it says.'

He placed an envelope in front of him, and Murad picked it up with trembling hands, nervously tearing it open to read it impatiently. It was brief in its message of flat refusal, warning that Athee not pursue the matter further. Murad took a deep breath as Mithal watched him.

'Do you remember your promise, Mithal?' he said.

'I do,' Mithal replied and then quickly asked, 'Do you trust me beyond a shadow of doubt?'

'I do,' Murad replied.

'You don't have any time left. I must tell you that Jannu has decided to wed his daughter to Bachal and the old hog will be coming the day after tomorrow for a formal ceremony. You have just a day to do what you want to,' Mithal said, nervously tapping the table.

'I am ready.' Murad was clear-minded in his response.

'Come to the thicket beside her home tomorrow at midnight. She will come to you when she hears your flute. Together you two will come to the old temple half a kilometre away. I will be waiting for you there. Do you understand?'

Murad pensively nodded his head and continued doing so for a while, bitter at the injustice of Marvi's parents. 'I will do that,' he told Mithal.

Mithal got up, shook his hand and left the cafe saying, 'We will meet again.'

When Murad entered his home, his demeanour troubled Athee. He had grown up in her lap and she could read his gestures and the creases on his forehead. But she left him to himself until he retired to bed. It was only then that Athee came and sat beside him.

Running her fingers through his hair, she gently asked, 'Won't you share it with me?'

Murad sat up in bed, disappointed in his inability to hide his feelings. 'It's about Marvi,' he said, and handed her the letter.

She glanced at the letter but didn't need to ask him to read it for her. 'They refused?' she asked.

Murad nodded his head in response. 'There is more. They have decided to wed her to a man a few years older than her father,' he told her.

'Bachal?' Athee asked softly.

'Yes,' Murad replied.

'That is worse than burying her alive,' she said sadly.

Murad then told her all about Mithal's promise to help them elope. 'I will have to save her, Athee, or she will kill herself.'

Athee sat silently, her head bent in contemplation. Finally, she raised her head to look at him. He was taken aback at the ferocity with which she spoke.

'I agree. You must,' she said decisively. 'This is now a matter of honour for us.'

Forty-four

Murad left his home early the next evening. Athee had only this to tell him: 'Don't be afraid. You have to be prepared to die if you want to live with dignity.' He then walked to his favourite mound outside the village and sat there to watch the sunset. He had always loved doing this. The sun descended to meet the earth, splashing a riot of colours across the horizon, juggling hues of red and grey in changing patterns. It was an evening like this that had kindled a love for the flute in him. He came regularly to pay homage to the display of beauty by playing his flute. That evening he saved his melody for Marvi and watched in silence.

Darkness descended quickly upon the quiet hamlet. As stars started twinkling in the night sky, the people of the village reciprocated by lighting lanterns in their homes. Murad shook his head at humanity's endless folly. He thought of fires in the hearths and homes rich with the aroma of baking bread. He imagined sleepy children struggling to stay awake and tired men stretching out on cots. He fondly thought of Athee too and wondered what she was doing. The time to start walking towards Marvi's home was drawing close. He pushed his thoughts away and summoned his courage for the task ahead. He planned to start his journey immediately after the evening call to prayer. He had to wait for just a few more minutes before the caller's voice rose into the night. The rise and fall of his voice, its trill and twirl and its undulating notes held him in thrall for as long as it reached his ears. When it ended, it was time to go.

~

Marvi had stayed aloof, feeling worthless since she overheard the conversation between her brother and parents. The home had lost its meaning for her and she felt insecure. She had spent the whole day languishing in the room waiting for night to fall. Nooran had treated her like a pariah, not even bothering to call her for food. Wali had left the house around noon saying he would return the next day. Jannu had gone loitering in the vacant villages and returned at dusk. He retired to his bed early after his dinner.

It was a hot and humid night, the kind that brings restless sleep and nightmares. Marvi, laying on her bed, feigned sleep but was wide awake, her heart pounding in her ears. She was scared. She had heard stories about girls losing their lives doing what she had resolved to do. Their blood was spilled for bringing dishonour to their families and they were buried in anonymous graves without a funeral or anyone to mourn them. Despite her fear of an ignominious death, she kept her resolve.

She waited through the long night, wondering why Murad was taking so long to come. It remained frustratingly silent except for the occasional seagull squawking across the sky. Even the dogs that barked at the passing of strangers seemed to have joined a conspiracy of silence. She was beginning to lose hope when she heard the flute. The sound rose and quickly died. She sat up in her bed and looked at her parents. Both of them were in a deep sleep. She slipped her feet into her shoes and wrapped a heavy shawl around her shoulders. She tiptoed towards the door, undid the latch and pulled it open gently. After one final look at the home she had grown up in, she stepped outside. The sound of the flute rose again, this time continuing for longer. She increased her speed, but a thorny bush caught her. She pulled at it frantically, tearing it in the effort and hastened forward, terrified that the sound of the flute would awaken her parents. The flute sounded again, louder this time. She started running. Suddenly, the sound of a single gunshot ripped through the silence of the night and the sound of the flute abruptly ceased.

Marvi froze in her path, horror-struck and paralysed.

'Murad!' she screamed in terror and scrambled forward, but someone grabbed her hair from behind and pulled her back.

'He is dead,' she heard in a harsh whisper.

When she turned her head, she saw Jannu's expressionless face, unfamiliar to her. She fell to her knees, her eyes fixed on the thicket in a catatonic stare.

Forty-five

Marvi stopped struggling and went limp in Jannu's arm, and he started to drag her desperate to take her away from the scene of the murder.

'Come on, you little wench,' he cursed her through clenched teeth.

Nooran came running to help him. Each holding one of her dainty wrists, they dragged her to the door. There Jannu picked her up and tossed her onto a cot. She was listless and dissociated, not uttering a single cry of pain or shedding a tear.

At daybreak, an anonymous caller informed the police about the murder on the lake. The officer in charge left for the scene of the crime with his small team. It included the policeman whom he had sent to warn Athee of the danger to her brother's life. They arrived in a pickup truck, where Mithal received them. He took them to the place where Murad's body lay, his flute broken and lying close by. His body was inspected and then covered with a sheet.

'It seems the lover boy met his fate. These things are not tolerated in our society,' Mithal remarked.

The officer in charge had been told about the identity of the deceased by his assistant, and he muttered something in agreement. He took time to inspect the scene of the crime. He noticed the telltale marks left by Jannu when he dragged Marvi away and the sight raised his hackles. He demanded to talk to the residents of the house, and Jannu and Nooran were called. They came running, nervous and short of breath. Both denied any knowledge of the incidence except the mayhem that woke them up.

'Who else lives in the house?' the officer asked, sitting down on the cot under the neem tree.

Mithal was quick to reply that Jannu's son and daughter also lived there. He called out loud for Wali, who appeared shortly after.

'The boy was with me the entire night,' Mithal told the officer who was about to question Marvi when Bachal arrived in his Land Cruiser.

The officer jumped to his feet and swiftly saluted him, his mind solving the puzzle in a flash as he recognized Bachal.

'So, what do you make of this mess?' Bachal asked him, not even honouring him with a direct look.

'It is obvious, sir. The boy was walking a forbidden path and was taken care of,' the officer quickly replied.

'By whom?' Bachal asked, this time looking straight into his eyes.

'I am afraid that will remain an unsolved mystery. There are no witnesses, no clues, nothing that can help us reach a conclusion,' the officer said, his head bent down.

'Well then, Mithal.' He addressed his servant, who jumped in obedience. 'Give them some money for a cup of tea on their way back.'

Mithal walked up to them, fumbling in his pockets for cash as they saluted him once more in unison.

Two hours later, when Murad's body had been removed and the police had finished their proceedings, a maulvi and a few women arrived in the tractor. They brought baskets of sweets and garlands with them. The women rushed to the house as Mithal started distributing the sweets. Marvi's face was painted and she was clad in a new red wedding dress. The wedding ceremony took place, during which Nooran pushed Marvi's head into a nod when she was asked for consent. The maulvi declared the wedding solemnized amidst loud cries of facilitation. A while later, Bachal escorted his bride to his gleaming vehicle, his hand firmly gripping Marvi's wrist. Marvi hadn't said a word or made a motion once during the charade.

Meanwhile, Wali had placed their belongings in the tractor trolley. He was handed the paper for the tractor and a transfer letter duly signed by Bachal. Nooran and Jannu walked up to Bachal to say goodbye to their daughter but could not dare to look at her. With their heads low, they begged Bachal to take care of her. Then, they boarded the tractor trolley. Wali was already behind the steering wheel. He waved his hand without looking and pressed the throttle. Black smoke billowed out of the exhaust pipe of the tractor and they were on their way.

The bride was made to sit on the front seat of Bachal's four-wheel drive. The maulvi and the women squeezed into the back seat. Bachal took the driver's seat and turned the ignition key. He knew that Mithal would follow on his motorcycle.

Mithal watched them leave with a victorious smile on his lips. He decided to sit on the cot and smoke a cigarette before leaving the place, never to return. His motorcycle was parked nearby. He looked up at the sky. There was still some time before dark, he could relax for a while. It had been a tiring, sleepless night. The sound of the tractor and Bachal's vehicle had dissipated in the vastness of the heath and an unsettling silence had returned. The wind whistled a gentle melancholy, interrupted only by the occasional call of a goose somewhere in the distance. As he blew wisps of smoke into the thick country air, he could see dusk was beginning to settle. He rose from the cot and walked towards his motorcycle. He turned to look back at the empty bush house one final time before he rode away. The air was still heavy with the telltale acrid smell of the water in the canal, which continued to flow.

Acknowledgements

I thank my children Saif, Kiran, Anum and Zain without whose encouragement I could not have told this story.

I thank Saif for typing, retyping and editing the script.

I thank my wife Zareen for her patience and support.

I also thank my friend Saleem Hussain for introducing me to Rupa Publications and pursuing the book on my behalf.

Finally, I am indebted to Rupa Publications for publishing this manuscript.